MIND
IS
GROUND
ZERO

• • • ● ● • • •

Outraged at the sight of his girlfriend's blood, David vented his anger on the gunman, scanning him relentlessly. Showing no mercy, harder and harder David concentrated his scan, almost enjoying the man's cries of pain.

David increased the power of his scan-tone, until it reached an ear-wrenching squeal. The criminal was paralyzed, his spinal cord ripping under the pressure. He writhed in the trap of the scanner's power. His head began to swell as the veins on the side of his temple turned blue. The scan turned the gunman's entire body into an electrical force, sending sparks of energy into the air.

The man's body exploded and the entire back of his head shattered, sending blood and gray brain matter splattering...

• • ● ● ● • • •

SCANNERS II

THE NEW ORDER

Professor Janus Kimball

A DOVE BOOK

WARNER BOOKS

A Time Warner Company

WARNER BOOKS EDITION

Warner Books, Inc.
666 Fifth Avenue
New York, NY 10103

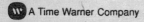 A Time Warner Company

Printed in the United States of America

First Printing: July, 1991

10 9 8 7 6 5 4 3 2 1

PROLOGUE

The following suicide note is in the City of Atlanta (Georgia) Police Department's case-file number SCX2-43802-M. The entire file plus certain effects of the late Dr. Jeffrey Hobgood are marked "Strictly Confidential, Security Access Only."

December 27, 1980

  I tried placing the gun several times to my head. It was the .38 caliber revolver which I had purchased in the mid-sixties when I first contemplated taking my own life. I couldn't do it then, and I found myself unable to do it now. I hadn't the courage to allow a bullet to impact against my skull with such speed and force that it shattered the bone and my brain beyond. Pills will be easier for me, I'm certain. I am about to take twelve Nembutals, six Halcions, and fourteen Dalmane capsules, their colorful assortment an artistic camouflage for their deadly assignment . . .

I've taken them now, washing them down with a glass of Crystal Champagne 1972. It was a gift from the late Dr. Paul Ruth. It is sweet irony that brings us together in death, for it was our unethical search into the limits of nature that brought me to this decision to end my life.

When I first met Dr. Ruth, he was a pioneer in the field of pharmacology. A brilliant man. How I envied his ability to restore health and provide sleep and comfort with the calculated combining of chemicals into drugs. By the age of thirty-six, he was already the president of Biocarbon Amalgamate and poised to announce what would be his greatest achievement—Ephemerol.

It was just after World War II. His excitement when he announced that he had developed a tranquilizer for pregnant women was understandable. "Smooth sailing," he said, even as he was giving the prototype of the drug to his own pregnant wife. He had no way of knowing that the drug had an invisible side effect: a nasty quirk of fate that somehow allowed the genes of unborn children to be affected, turning them into what we would later label scanners.

When Dr. Ruth's first son was born, he looked so normal. A healthy baby boy with an intense curiosity for life. After his wife became pregnant a second time, it seemed perfectly safe to allow her to take Ephemerol again. In fact, this time he even increased her dosage.

It took several years before Dr. Ruth realized that his sons were different from the other children. They had this uncanny ability to control people with their minds. They began to hear voices, to unconsciously read people's minds until they were unable to stop the sounds bombarding their brains.

A gift, yet a curse; it was at once horrible, yet fascinating to Dr. Ruth. He found himself studying his sons like laboratory animals, testing their blood, testing their minds. The strain was too much for his wife, who died while receiving shock treatments in a mental hospital in 1972.

My fascination with his experiments grew right from the start, developing into a morbid thirst for every shred of new information which Dr. Ruth could provide about the telepathic abilities of his sons. When he began to sense that my interest went deeper than friendly concern, however, he cut me off from his lab and tempered our friendship. Perhaps it was a father's instinctive protective nature.

After I learned that there were many other scanners born as a result of Ruth's drug-testing program, my interest compounded. I was not to be stopped. I wanted to learn how to harness this telepathic power and use it for mankind. As chairman of Con-Sec Corporation, I had the power to make my desires reality. It mattered little that Con-Sec was an international security conglomerate which specialized in providing private armies to foreign nations. The power to control people had endless potential.

Moving quickly, I arranged to purchase Ruth's Biocarbon Amalgamate. And with it, I bought Dr. Ruth himself. He became a pawn in my desire for world power under the guise of Ephemerol research. Slowly, we began to make contact with other scanners throughout the country and to network them together in an effort to understand their powers more clearly.

Dr. Ruth had discovered that Ephemerol could be used to control the mental imbalance of his sons and other scanners, just as it had created their unique power. Yet the boys were kept separated at all times, never interacting. We feared their combined power.

The brothers were even given separate identities so that no future association could be made. The older was named Darryl Revok; the younger Cameron Vale. By the time Darryl was eighteen, he was already out of control, having drilled a half-inch hole in the center of his skull to "let the voices out."

It became obvious as Darryl became older that he was crazy, his mind a sickened, distorted testing ground. Eventually, he rebelled against his father, who continued to refuse him any contact with his brother and denied him a life outside of the laboratory.

I admit now, as my own mind weakens and begins to grow vague with the redeeming cloud of sleep, that I encouraged Revok's rebellion. He had a plan. One that would do more than just collect together an underground of scanners, now several hundred in number and scattered throughout the country. Revok's plan was to deliberately create more scanners, an entire army of scanners, by using a handful of doctors who would deliberately inject unsuspecting pregnant women with Ephemerol.

Do not judge me too harshly. It's true that I supplied Revok with the money to produce the Ephemerol drug by the tankful. And I used Con-Sec's security contacts to coerce doctors to cooperate with Revok's plan. But you must understand. It was for the future generations of the world that I donated my resources to this cause.

I could not have known that Revok would annihilate any scanner who refused to cooperate with his plan—the death squads that would gun down civilians and scanners alike. I could not have known.

And who at Con-Sec could have predicted the ultimate

tragedy that took place when Revok confronted his brother Cameron for the first time. The personal war that erupted when Cameron refused to join his brother in his plot to replicate his own kind; and the resulting chaos that ensued when Cameron's mind and ethics were sucked into Darryl's body in the ultimate scanning duel.

I have called scanners "telepathic curiosities." For that I am sorry. They are geniuses beyond all else. It was Revok, not me, that caused the killing.

I must confess that I did nothing to stop the assassination of Dr. Paul Ruth when he tried to interfere with our plans. I continued to run Con-Sec as if everything was business-as-usual. But the authorities would not stop their continual investigations. Their harassment was endless.

My head is so heavy now. The drugs make it nearly impossible to see the page. The pressure that has grown over the past years will finally be forgiven by the kindness of death.

For those who remain to laugh and sing after my body is discovered, I remind you of one thing. Scanners are all-powerful, all-knowing. They are now everywhere. Behold with respect these special people, yet beware their pledge of sanity.

The body of Dr. Jeffrey Hobgood, chairman emeritus of the Con-Sec Corporation, was discovered on December 30, 1980, by his cleaning lady. Several empty prescription bottles were on the floor beside his body. Hardened with rigor mortis, his hand clutched a vial of Ephemerol.

CHAPTER ONE

DRAK

Fallmount Mental Health Sanitarium, Psychological Profile:
STEVEN DRAK

*Subject is a 5' 10" male caucasian with a history of mental
disorders. First reported hospitalization: January 14, 1974,
Bolford Psychiatric Clinic, Scarsdale, New York. Diag-
nosed schizophrenic.*

Comments:
*Steven Drak should be regarded as hostile and dan-
gerous. Despite repeated hypnotherapy and electroconvul-*

7

sive therapy, Drak has shown progressive mood swings and extreme social withdrawal. His medical history lists a concussion to the parietal lobe of the brain at the age of five. Police reports suggest physical abuse, although no charges were filed at the time. On varying occasions, Drak has explained the incident as either a fall from a horse or a fall from a bike. He makes no mention of the repeated physical beatings at the hands of his parents which caused his removal to the custody of foster homes at the age of seven. Both his parents subsequently died under mysterious circumstances, with suicide listed as the official cause of death by the Bronx (NY) County Coroner's office.

Drak's emotional swings have made educational alternatives extremely limited, with his current formal education ending during the seventh grade. Because of a violent temper and learning disabilities, Drak was placed in a state-run reform school by government authorities eager to teach him discipline. Over the next six years, he was transferred between the Overton Correctional Institution, the Larchmont School for Disadvantaged Youths, the Brownsville Home (a reformatory operated under the auspices of the United Methodist Church), and the New York State Juvenile Correctional Institution at Hampstead. In each case, Drak displayed an unwillingness to cooperate with authorities, and escaped from custody eighteen times within a four-year period.

In 1974, he was brought to the maximum security ward of the Bolford Psychiatric Clinic for observation and treatment after escaping for the final time from the Brownsville Home. Earlier that same day, a fire destroyed Brownsville, resulting in the death of three children under the age of ten, with sixteen serious injuries to others. Arson was confirmed, and while Drak was never formally charged with the crime, he was the chief suspect at the time of his hos-

pitalization. During the subsequent three years, Drak was kept in solitary confinement, and underwent extensive testing to determine the cause and extent of his schizophrenia. Noted psychotherapist Dr. Marian Robinson was placed in charge of Drak's treatment, which included the experimental antidepressant drug, CO15. Dr. Robinson credits much of her success with Drak to this drug, despite its severe side effects including nausea, abnormal heartbeat, and damage to kidneys. In 1978, Drak was transferred to the Fallmount Mental Health Sanitarium, a minimum-security facility where Drak's condition progressively improved although he continued to complain of hearing voices and conversations within his head. He was assigned duties as a groundsman and displayed a fondness for flowers and landscaping. Six days before his scheduled release from Fallmount, Steven Drak disappeared from the facility. Security guards subsequently found that the lock on a storage closet had been forced open, its contents, uniforms worn by the Fallmount janitorial staff, had been removed. Steven Drak's current condition and whereabouts are unknown.

(Signed)
Dr. Timothy Mathias

A solitary cat searching through the decaying trash from the Twin Dragon All-Nite Chinese Emporium and Deli heard it first. It stiffened to attention at the faintest sound of shuffling. Not the echoing click of heels on the potholed macadam, but a strange, erratic lunging of feet before body. As the cat prepared to jump to safety, all was quiet again. Only the distant sound of a police siren and the continuing drone of traffic on the bustling street beyond pierced the night air. Its curiosity satisfied, the black feline licked its tail, oblivious to the danger a heartbeat away.

Steven Drak paused at the entrance to the alleyway,

partially hidden in a long-unused doorway covered in soot from years of city exhaust. Puddles in the street reflected the look of torment in his eyes. Suddenly, he let out a silent yell as he bolted against the door as if to burst through in spontaneous revolt. Again he tried; again he failed as his muscular, stocky body crumbled to the pavement in obvious defeat.

His long hair was greased and tangled, his beard showing the stubble of life on the run. Ripping at his temples, he screamed at the sounds within his head—voices, sirens, and street noises, all part of high-pitched city life, were magnified a thousand-fold as they rang inside his brain.

"Stop!" Drak commanded. "Stop," he pleaded, his bulging eyes glistening with the glazed look of a madman trying unsuccessfully to control his mind. He was doubled over in pain, as the pressure built until sound would no longer come from his lips.

Wrestling to his feet like a caged animal, Drak lunged forward, knocking over several empty trash cans, and rotated into the darkened alley. The black cat had long since cleared the way for Drak's arrival, as he half-stumbled, half-ran, clenching his temples in pain.

He collapsed on a filthy sewer grate, the sound of running water diverting his thoughts, and suddenly the voices stopped. Drak gulped for air in obvious appreciation, inhaling the dirty oxygen and heaving to expel it from his lungs.

How much longer could he take this living hell? The sounds were growing louder and louder with each passing day. His eyes were ready to burst from their sockets like a safety value on an overheated pressure cooker. A nightmare from which there was only fleeting escape.

Slowly rising to his feet, Drak attempted to smooth out his shirt, stained from life on the run and vile perspiration.

How long had it been, he tried to remember, since he bathed or changed or slept like normal human beings? How long since he felt the warmth of another person close to his body, now caked with days of sleeping in doorways and half-full dumpsters?

The sudden intrusion of a police car in the alley turned momentary relief into sudden paranoia. He couldn't be caught; not here, not now.

Run! his mind silently screamed.

Pushing past boxes of garbage smelling of day-old fish, Drak inched along the damp walls, hoping to escape the slowly advancing searchlight scouring the alley for signs of life.

The bright beam sent Drak into a race against time. Darting into the light, he pushed himself into a sprint, gulping at the air to gain strength.

Move, move, MOVE, his mind directed his feet.

His heart beating wildly, Drak lunged around the corner just as the policeman turned his attention toward the fleeing stranger. And by the time the cop had accelerated and reached the alley's end, Drak had long since escaped into the night.

Slamming the door behind him, Drak found himself in a crowded video arcade. The kind that had sprung up on every other block in this neighborhood of street gangs and late-hour fast-food hangouts.

The Video Playcade was different however. It prided itself on having the very latest games available. From high-tech laser-controlled action games to electronic pinball, Playcade was state-of-the-art, and its newest, most challenging game of all was Destroyer.

The line of kids and adults alike waiting for their chance at the elaborate glass and chrome machine with the synthetic voice and laserbeam controls stretched almost to the door.

Hearing the cheers of excitement and the sounds of destruction on the game's screen, the insidious child in Drak was aroused.

Pushing past the crowd despite their protests, Drak watched with alert senses and interest as the current player was destroyed by the military monster screaming in victory. Drak could do better, and intended to try.

"Hey, scumbag," the tough-looking kid who was next in line shouted at Drak as he grabbed the controls. "I'm next here," he slurred, cocking his head so that his earring dangled in mock display.

"Not now, you ain't," Drak snarled back, shoving the kid back into the mass of people.

Ignoring the shouts of the startled crowd, Drak dropped his quarter in the coin slot and prepared for war. Flexing his shoulders and grabbing the controls, he began to fly his Destroyer craft over the alien terrain as the game lit up in action. Mesmerized, he aimed and hit target after target, blowing up alien cities with a newfound talent that amazed even him.

Feeling a sense of control and power, Drak moved his craft faster and faster across the screen, blasting everything in his path with unerring accuracy. As the now-silenced group of teenagers and adults looked on in disbelief, Drak cackled in triumph, feeling as if he were on stage, the center of attention and loving the sensation.

He was in his glory, thrust into the limelight as the sounds of violent electronic explosions pierced the air. Determined to test himself and gain long overdue self-gratification, Drak dramatically released the game's hand control.

The gasp from the gawking onlookers was food for Drak's ego. Taking control telekinetically, Drak accelerated the game even faster than before. The scoring mechanism began to spin out of control as Drak hit his mark again and again.

As the fantasy terrain rolled by, the monster that beat the last player was nowhere to be seen. Or was it? The game was progressing so rapidly now that the screen turned into a blur of light and sound. Suddenly sparks began to fly from under the glass screen as an arid wisp of smoke rose from the Destroyer gameboard.

Faster, faster, Drak's thoughts descended upon the video screen as the sounds of electronic noise began to scream into the air. The unwanted intrusions of too many eyes, too many minds, began to make their voices known. The cries from the surrounding crowd made Drak's eyes bulge and his veins pulse as his face turned into a distorted caricature of pain.

It was then that Playcade's hefty security guard made his presence known, unaware of the power within this unwanted intruder. Feeling a strong hand on his shoulder, Drak spun in defense, clearing all his thoughts of play and concentrating on attack.

Eyes bugging out of their sockets, the challenge was clear: Attack or be captured. Without hesitation, Drak scanned the security guard with an intensity previously reserved for late-night experimentation.

Slammed into the Destroyer game with brutal accuracy, the otherwise-untouched guard shook his head in disbelief. His attacker had done nothing more than stare in his direction.

The gathered teens dropped their street-tough composure, scattering in all directions as Drak ran across the game room toward the door. The echo of the guard shouting for the police drifted after him in useless pursuit.

One last message. One last reminder of his power. Drak snapped his head and with a concentrated show of scan-force made short work of the video games still playing their electronic serenades. In a final ferocious scan-burst, the room lit up in a medley of sparks and explosions. With that, Drak disappeared.

Police Commander Wayne Forrester got the call about twenty minutes later. A little too thick around the middle, Forrester was a veteran cop with unsatisfied political aspirations. There was nothing in his personality that allowed for humor; even less that tolerated romance. The very fact that he was still at his desk at two A.M. more than attested to the fact. His hawkish face snapped to attention; his flaming red hair stood on end as he got the news.

"Forrester," he said gruffly as he grabbed at the receiver.

"We've found another one, Chief," came the reply from his main operative, Guy Gelson. The plainclothes detective was speeding through the city in his unmarked cruiser. Thick-necked, beefy, crewcut Gelson licked his lips nervously as he talked into his cellular phone.

A onetime marine, Gelson had the look of a bulldog, a fact which prompted his nickname Spike. Never to his face, of course; his temper being as quick as his fists. And at the moment, Spike was on the scent.

"We sure as hell found another one," he howled, a little dribble edging out of the corner of his mouth.

"You sure?" doubted Forrester, having been fooled too many times in the past. "You better be damn sure this time, Gelson," he added, narrowing his steely eyes in anticipation of triumph.

"He just trashed an arcade full of video machines without touching 'em, that's all, Chief! Sure enough sounds like one to me," Gelson smiled, suddenly turning his attention to his driving as he narrowly missed an old garbage can which had rolled into the street. "Those damn dogs," he muttered before realizing that the boss was still listening intently on the line. "So, Chief, two of our men chased this guy into Rich Brothers warehouse. You know, the department store on Thirty-seventh?"

A sardonic glaze came across Forrester's eyes. "Keep this off the airwaves. I'm on my way," he said before dropping the phone back on its cradle.

Grabbing his topcoat, Forrester wrestled to get his arm hurriedly into the sleeve. A little too tailored for the broad-chested policeman, it rippled across the back as he jostled his body into its winter wrap. Finding a pack of cigarettes in the pocket, he lit one up absentmindedly, oblivious to a habit which had taken twelve years to develop. Without sitting down, he punched a button on his telephone and the sounds of an automatic dialer played a short tune in the air.

Dr. Gareth Morse was working late as usual in his high-tech lab at the institute. The darkness around him served to highlight the glare from the halogen lamp currently aimed at his lab table.

He removed some yellow liquid from an ampule marked *EPH-2* and placed it gently on a slide. Morse's nerves were shot. The shaking of his hands as he tried to manipulate the slide under the microscope proved the point. So did the gray, drawn skin under his eyes.

Lately, he had been working too hard, too long, he realized. But it was work that was essential to save lives. The wall in front of him was stacked floor to ceiling with the failed results of similar tests. Each ampule of *EPH-2* was neatly labeled in its own place on the wall, a testament to his trial-and-error experiments which had occupied his life for the past five years.

He ignored the ringing of his wall phone for as long

as he could. Finally, nerves and the constant whining of the electronic tone prompted him to lift the telephone receiver. He pulled down his surgical mask to speak.

"What is it," he growled, obviously disturbed. The message he was hearing was worth the interruption; the tension drained from his face and a hint of a smile glimmered on his lips. "I'm on my way," was his only comment before hanging up the phone, locking his current experiment in his safe, and rushing from the lab. The halogen lamp cast its eerie glow as the solitary sentry.

The glare from police spotlights had an entirely different effect when they hit the wall of the Rich Brothers warehouse. The old brick building had been painted with advertisements over the years; the slogans peeling, only to be replaced with new, improved products and services. A portion of an ad for a locksmith seemed to be peeking out from behind the current advertisement for a candy that "melted in your mouth." And now, in the bright glare of the spotlights, their assorted messages seemed to be leaping forth in an effort to attract attention.

As Lieutenant Gelson pulled up outside the warehouse, two young officers were already out of their cars, shotguns pointed in the direction of the building. Gelson silently signalled them to move their spotlights off the wall and toward a broken warehouse window just thirty yards away. Only after Gelson moved to take cover beside them did he dare speak.

"What the hell's he doing in there?" he asked, responding to what sounded like the screaming of a trapped wild animal.

"Can't figure it out," the younger of the two patrolmen answered. "We cornered him in there and then he started to rip the place apart. This guy nuts or what?"

"Block off both ends of the street," Gelson replied,

ignoring the question. He knew all too well how dangerous his captive creature was. This time he wasn't leaving anything to chance. Too many times in the past he had been in this exact situation of having a perfect specimen, cornered and ripe for capture, only to misjudge events and lose his prey.

Inside the dark warehouse, Drak was a madman on a rampage. The thick layer of dust covering old mannequins and crates formed an otherworldly smoke screen in the air as light from the spotlights leaked through the shattered window.

He smashed anything and everything in his path. Unable to handle his impending doom, he was reduced to a salivating creature, trapped by his own past and afraid of his own future.

"Shut up, *SHUT UP!*" he screamed, grabbing at another wooden crate and heaving it toward a silent and unseen enemy. "Leave me alone . . . I said, leave me alone, . . . No, don't come in here . . . Damn you . . . *LEAVE ME ALONE!*"

Deteriorating into a neanderthal position and swinging his arms like a mountain gorilla, Drak was a man possessed. He recklessly jumped on top of a pile of old supplies covered by a tarpaulin damp with mildew, all the while continuing his verbal rampage.

When he spotted a pair of naked mannequins in the corner, their eyes scorching him with their unblinking gaze, he recoiled in terror, clawing at the tarp trying to hide himself.

"Don't look at me. You're not allowed to look at me," he screamed.

Reaching for a long pole, Drak began to swing it over his head in helicopter fashion, sending heads and arms of mannequins smashing to the ground.

Outside, Wayne Forrester's shiny Buick sedan inched past the young patrolman who had set up a temporary roadblock at the end of Thirty-seventh Street. Despite the late hour, several dozen of the town's more curious residents had begun to gather, attracted by the flashing lights on the police car and the sound of destruction muted in the distance.

"Get these jerks out of here," Forrester growled at the young rookie as he passed, pointing in the direction of several winos sitting on the curb, bottles in hand.

Seeing Forrester approach, Gelson began to glow that warm smile of someone who knows he's done well and is about to be congratulated. But the police commander wasn't in a complimenting mood. He had seen this kind of operation fall apart in seconds before.

"He's in there. Hear him?" Gelson asked, like a schoolkid fearing his teacher.

"The whole town hears him, Gelson," Forrester snapped back. "Why don't we just invite the news crews in here and really announce our little operation."

As if on cue, Drak sent his own greeting their way. He had picked up a mannequin and sent it hurtling through the window. Its silhouette in the spotlight had the appearance of a suicide victim falling to his death. Perhaps it was an omen of things to come.

Moments later, Dr. Morse's BMW rolled across broken glass and twigs as he turned off the road and pulled up alongside the police cars just as a paramedic's ambulance blared its own arrival.

"Cut the siren!" Forrester barked, staring a silent hello to Dr. Morse.

"Feck. Gruner!" Morse shouted at the ambulance when the sound continued.

Instantly, the siren was quieted; the headlights were doused as the two uniformed paramedics leapt out of the ambulance. It would be hard to decide which one appeared the more strange.

Feck was tall. But not an attractive tall. Rather that too spindly, reed-thin kind of physique associated with basketball players. His cruel, sunken eyes had a desperate look—scary, haunted, to be avoided at all costs.

Gruner was merely ugly. The stronger of the pair, his horrible complexion set the tone for his entire appearance. A pockmarked balding man with rotten teeth and a nervous facial tic.

Carrying metal cases, the pair quickly approached Forrester.

"Scanners?" the Police Commander asked Morse, who nodded in response. "Can they handle this?"

Without answering, Dr. Morse snapped his fingers toward Feck and Gruner, who instinctively set their cases down and removed scoped, state-of-the-art automatic tranquilizer dart rifles.

"Nembutal boosters," Morse informed Forrester. "We want him unharmed."

Nodding in agreement, Feck and Gruner obeyed, loading full clips of darts in their rifles, a little too mechanically for humans with a soul.

Gelson, still maintaining his cover behind the door of one squad car, slowly removed a flash grenade and prepared it for firing.

The intense activity outside the warehouse ran counter to the increasing sounds of horror within. Drak moved like a mad dog now, pacing back and forth underneath the window. Occasionally, as if fearing his own shadow, he would react to his reflection and crouch in the darkness. Only his tormented panting broke the silence.

Then, just as unexpectedly, he would leap to action, shattering more mannequins in his path. Confusion saturated his mind as he moved to the window, his eyes burning hatefully. Glaring out from the shattered glass, he attempted to focus a scan.

Forrester was hit suddenly by an invisible force which lifted him off the ground and hurled him backward into the dust. It was a paralyzing jolt; he could hardly breathe as he staggered back to the stunned crowd, gasping for air.

"Shit . . . Morse!" he ached out from his throat.

Holding onto the car door, he felt his heart beating in bursts and starts. His entire body tingled in an afterscan of incredible pain. His blood seemed to be charged with electricity and pulsed through his veins at an incredible speed.

Helping the police commander up, Dr. Morse was smiling—hardly the reaction Forrester had expected. Pulling the ailing policeman behind the protection of the car door, Morse gently wiped blood from Forrester's nostrils.

"He scanned you from thirty yards. Pretty impressive," Morse commented with scientific detachment, obviously impressed by Drak's achievement.

Forrester tried to talk, but could only grimace in pain.

With an echoing thud, the rookie patrolmen sprung the giant metal warehouse door open. Drak spun in surprise, rising to his feet and howling in terror. Gelson, armed and waiting, fired a flash grenade, which exploded in blinding brightness. For Drak, the hopelessness of his situation was not yet obvious. He recoiled in fear while covering his eyes from the brilliant light.

"Take him," Gelson yelled, the adrenaline pumping faster now as Drak began to move. "Take him, you idiots," he repeated, afraid to waste the element of surprise.

Gruner was the first to move, racing toward Drak with his tranquilizer rifle ready to fire. Heart racing toward his prey, he realized he had to shoot before Drak could regain his sense of direction.

Too late. With uncanny accuracy, Drak was spinning around even as Gruner was beginning his charge. With an intensity that belied the wickedness he felt, Drak scanned his challenger, roaring madly in triumph. As Gruner fell to the ground, convulsing uncontrollably, he shot wildly into the air, his tranquilizer dart barely missing Gelson.

"Fool," Feck hissed from his bunker behind some splintered crates.

Taking aim, Feck fired—once, then twice. Drak aimed a scan in his direction, but he was too late. Even as he focused on his attacker, he felt the sting of tranquilizer darts in his neck and chest. Yanking at them furiously, Drak began to feel their effect as the drug hit his bloodstream.

Stumbling backward past the rumble of his earlier destruction, he somehow made it to the warehouse door. The cool night air acted as a stimulant, but only briefly. As he looked up and moaned, he felt his body crumbling to the soft grass below.

David Ketchum had little tolerance for traffic. Born on a farm in Vermont, he had only recently migrated to the big city to attend college, and as he sat, stalled in rush-hour traffic, he longed to walk through his favorite pasture, to be at one with nature. His love of animals had been such an important part of his life that a career as a veterinarian seemed ideal for the twenty-four-year-old.

Handsome in an uncalculated way, the country boy flexed his body—stiff from too many minutes of bumper-to-bumper traffic. His old pickup truck, still caked with Vermont mud on its plates, was equally unhappy with the challenge of city driving. A quick glance at the temperature gauge proved the point, and David knew he had to free them both.

He turned the wheel sharply to the right and the four-wheeler bounced over the curb onto the sidewalk as shoppers screamed and laughed in equal proportion. David was moving now, sidestepping the traffic and feeling the breeze against his face.

He knew he was late for class. Really late. Since there was no real need for a watch in the country, he relied on instinct to determine the time, and his instinct told him that he was in big trouble. As he snapped on the radio, he barely missed hitting a mailbox and somehow did hit a trash can, spewing paper cups and newspapers across the sidewalk behind him.

". . . foresee increasing population density, worsening traffic, environmental problems, as well as stress-related illnesses," the radio announcer was saying.

David smiled as he maneuvered his truck off the sidewalk and back onto the street. "All right!" he rejoiced as he saw a clear road ahead. "Let's move it, Myrtle, let's move it," he laughed, talking to his truck and hitting the accelerator.

"On the local scene, police still have no suspects in the Milk Murderer Tampering Case. So far, two children have died of strychnine poisoning while a third remains in serious condition," David's radio blared. He pulled into a parking spot on the crowded campus lot and leapt from the cab, book-bag in hand.

"Remind me to cut down on milk," he thought, racing across the manicured lawn and into the medical building, pausing just long enough to smell a special jasmine plant he particularly enjoyed.

Retrieving a surgical gown from the sterile laundry room, David made his way into the operating room where Dr. Mumford was performing surgery on a dog with a ruptured spleen. Not one of David's favorite courses. In fact, the idea of cutting into an animal strapped to a table made him feel quite uncomfortable, and he didn't hesitate to avoid operating lab if he could. Today was not one of those days.

"Sorry I'm late," he whispered as he moved in between eight other students, all wearing gowns and masks.

The look white-haired old Mumford shot in his direction removed any hope of forgiveness. Accepting a scalpel from his medical assistant, Dr. Mumford continued his explanation of migratory thrombophlebitis, a precancerous condition common in animals and humans.

David was trying to concentrate. Really, he was. But it was difficult with Alice Leonardo standing so near him.

"Even in a surgical mask, she's special," David found himself thinking as he lost himself in her bright blue eyes. Though they had never been formally introduced, David felt very close to Alice as he watched her in class. Her long, silky brown hair glistened in the reflection of the surgical lamp, and it wasn't until she spoke that David realized he must have been quite obvious with his stare.

"You missed all the fun," she whispered in his direction.

David felt himself blushing as he turned his attention back to Dr. Mumford, who was now beginning to remove the injured spleen from the black labrador retriever. The lab assistant was busy handing the surgeon an array of equipment and instruments. He clamped off the blood as it began to ooze from the incision, staining his lab jacket and operating table sheets as he progressed.

With every slice of the scalpel, Dr. Mumford had a dramatic explanation of the implications of each cut. Alice was used to his melodramatic instruction, having been in surgery with Dr. Mumford before. She couldn't help smiling as he exaggerated every move, waving a surgical clamp in the air as he spoke.

Ready to break into laughter, she turned to David to

see if he found it as funny as she did. His eyes were closed and the first signs of tiny sweat beads were beginning to form across his brow. Clearly he was feeling ill.

"Are you all right," she whispered with genuine concern.

"I . . . I'm sorta . . . Excuse me, please," David stuttered, grabbing his mouth and hurrying quietly from the room. Alice was only one step behind.

Removing her surgical mask, Alice raced to his side in the waiting room. Her beauty was more apparent now, out of the harsh bright light of surgery. Her skin had an alabaster glow, flawless in its smooth luminescence. Her blue-violet eyes had the warmth that only caring can bring—and a certain mischievousness which became even more visible as she spoke.

"What's the matter, David. You're not a bit squeamish, are you?" she teased.

Rubbing his temples and trying to catch his breath, David could hardly respond. "I . . . No, not really. I've just . . . Well, I've just been having these strange headaches lately," he confessed.

"Ah, poor baby," Alice teased, massaging the top of his shoulders.

At the moment of her touch, David tensed—finally pulling away from her and walking across the room to a puppy who was quivering in the bottom of a small cage. Stricken with a neurological disease, the young spaniel was in obvious pain.

"At least you don't have canine encephalitis, like this little guy," Alice said, following him across the room. "Look at this poor baby."

David watched with admiration as Alice opened the cage and without hesitating gently pulled the puppy into her arms, cradling it like a baby and stroking its head gently. Despite its agony, the puppy obviously was enjoying the attention and love.

"They'll probably put him to sleep after they've finished experimenting," Alice admitted sadly. "It's probably just as well."

There was a tear of compassion in David's eyes as he watched the dog shiver uncontrollably in her arms. Putting out his hands, he gently took the dog from Alice and comfortably placed it on the sofa in the waiting room. Slowly, he began to stroke its spine, concentrating his stare on the movement of his hands.

Alice watched in amazement as the dog gradually relaxed its body and brought its quiver under control. Her training told her that nothing could improve this dog's condition, yet her eyes saw an improvement beyond comprehension.

Turning her attention back to David, she noticed he was muttering some sort of chant, barely audible under his breath. His eyes were practically shut in a trance. In fact, he actually seemed to be feeling this dog's pain and absorbing its fatal affliction.

Feeling Alice's stare, David smiled gently and spoke quietly to the puppy as he continued his quiet stroking. "Don't worry, buddy. You're going to be all right. Just be a good boy and we'll get you out of here."

As David placed the dog back in its cage, Alice stared at David in amazement. Incredulous, she tried to speak.

Smiling his cutest countryboy grin, David offered no explanation other than admitting that he had a way with animals.

Who is this strange, wonderful person, Alice thought, as she followed him outside and across the parking lot. He had only been in school for several weeks, and they never really had a chance to talk about anything other than homework or lab assignments.

"I've never asked you where you're from, David," Alice said with a curious look as she tried her best to match his broad, swift stride.

"Richfalls, Vermont," David answered easily. "My parents have a farm. I've only been gone a few weeks, and I already miss it."

"So, you don't like the city much, huh?"

"What's there to like," David answered sharply, a slight tone of irritation creeping into the conversation for the first time. "Where I come from, there's rolling green hills and a tiny brook that never runs dry. Not even in the coldest winter. And there's so many stars in the sky at night that you could spend a lifetime and never hope to see them all. Around here, you have to look to find a green tree, or even a patch of wall without graffiti. About the only thing that's plentiful in this place is noise. Noise and traffic and the pollution! Sometimes I can't even breathe . . ."

Given the quality of air in cities these days, the idea wasn't without merit, Alice thought. "Who needs to breathe when you meet so many interesting people?" she answered facetiously.

"Too many people," David impulsively responded, totally missing her point.

"What about friends, David," she asked. "Don't you have any friends here?"

"Not really," he answered, shaking his head and avoiding her eyes.

"Well, I'll be your friend," Alice offered, stopping in her tracks and holding out her hand toward him. "I'll be your friend if you'd like, David."

Tentatively accepting her hand in his own, David

wasn't sure what she wanted, or exactly what she was saying. "Alice Leonardo, like the artist," she continued as his hand met hers. "Tonight, maybe we could do something . . ." Alice started to say, but stopped as David pulled back, retreating into his shell.

Beginning to walk again, he didn't even look back, hoping she wouldn't follow. Yet, as he reached his truck, Alice was right behind, touching his shoulder and calling his name.

"Look. Alice. Thanks but no thanks. You're very nice, but I really have got to get back to my dorm. I have to start cramming. You know, that pathology assignment, and I missed today's surgery."

Alice stopped him with a slender index finger against his lips. "Studying pathology on a Friday night, David, is pathological. You have to have some fun. That's what this doctor orders," she smiled, not about to take no for an answer.

"You're only a vet," David reminded her, not knowing what else to say. He felt the redness of a blush beginning to boil across his face again.

If it showed, Alice chose to ignore it. "And not for another four years," she added. "But certain remedies work across species you know," she continued to tease.

Picking up on her mood, David asked, "And what species am I?"

"We'll get to that later, farm boy," she winked. "For now, how about some Italian food."

David had never met a woman quite like Alice. He wanted to say yes to her obvious advances, but found himself intimidated by his own secrets. "No, look, I told you before, I'm falling behind," he abruptly said, opening his truck door and beginning to climb in. "I've gotta go."

"Okay, if you don't want to," Alice said, challenging

him without backing away. David looked into her eyes and
knew he couldn't say no, yet shouldn't say yes. "What do
you have to lose?" Alice continued relentlessly.

He looked deeply into Alice's eyes, unintentionally
scanning her thoughts for the first time. Suddenly, he relaxed, at last convinced that this girl meant no harm and
wasn't a threat.

"I guess I don't have *anything* to lose," he said after
what seemed an interminably long pause.

"You live in Radwell?" she asked. He nodded. "I'll
pick you up at eight. Dress to impress."

Then she turned and walked away. David watched the
gentle sway of her narrow hips as she rounded the corner
of the parking lot and disappeared from view. The smile
on David's lips grew wider as he dreamed of the night ahead.
Yet, as he steered his truck out on to the main highway, a
sudden darkness crossed his face as self-doubt and long-
subdued fears surfaced within his mind.

CHAPTER TWO

ALICE

Application for admission, Thorndyke Veterinary College
DAVID KETCHUM

Gentlemen:

As a recent graduate of Marlboro College, Marlboro, Vermont, with a cumulative grade point average of 3.75, I would like to be considered for admission to Thorndyke Veterinary College. As requested, I have enclosed notarized copies of my transcripts, as well as the following background brief.

As a student at Marlboro College, I majored in biology,

*and was a member of the wrestling team and the National
Honor Society. I was also active in the Vermont State Farm
Association drive to eradicate hoof-and-mouth disease from
the New England states.*

*Having grown up on a 2400-acre farm in southern
Vermont, I was surrounded by animals my entire life. My
earliest memories are flooded with the antics of cattle and
horses which my family and I raised. Even before entering
grade school, I was active with our local 4-H club and
began working with our local veterinarian, Dr. Mitchell
Hall. It is my life's goal to return to this community and
take over Dr. Hall's practice upon his retirement.*

*To this end I respectfully request consideration for
admission to Thorndyke which will provide me with the
valuable training that I will so desperately need.*

Respectfully,
David Ketchum

Dr. Morse reached for the beeper on his belt and
quickly glanced at its message before dropping it in the
pocket of his white coat and rushing toward the elevator at
the end of the hall.

He could feel drops of perspiration running from his
armpits down the inside of his short-sleeve shirt. It was a
natural reaction, he thought. This would be a big day. It
was all right to be excited.

How long he had waited for another chance to find the
answer. How long it had been before he had found someone
with the power of Steven Drak. He could feel victory this
time, putting years of failure out of his mind and concentrating on the challenge that lay ahead.

Pounding on the elevator button, Morse cursed its slow
speed. He pounded again, and at last the door opened with
a slight grating sound.

Once he was inside the elevator, the soft droning of the lifting mechanism was gradually overtaken by a noise that increased in intensity as the elevator arrived at the ground floor of the Institute Testing Lab. The sound was haggard and obviously out of control. An animal trapped by its own fear.

Steven Drak was wailing in anger, his tortured face only calming down long enough to spit into the face of Police Commander Forrester as he attempted to restrain the man-beast in a chair. Still recovering from the effect of the tranquilizer darts, Drak nevertheless had enough strength to fight being held in a strange place against his will.

Dr. Morse raced toward Drak's cries down the dim basement corridor, past door after door of observation rooms, until he finally hastily punched his security code into the panel next to the last doorway.

"Stop it!" Morse yelled as Forrester slapped Drak across the face hard enough to cut his lip. "Stop it, you idiot!" he continued his tirade, pulling Forrester away from his incredibly strong patient. "Don't you realize what this man could do to you with very little instigation, you fool?"

Forrester was obviously not used to be being talked to in such a fashion, but under the circumstances, he held his temper and his comments, instead backing away and allowing Morse full access to Steven Drak. From across the room, Feck had moved closer, a tranquilizer gun in his hand, ready for any emergency.

"Relax, Steven," Dr. Morse instructed in a gentle voice, attempting to calm the savage man. Ignoring Drak's wails and his continuing struggle against his chair restraints, Morse remained soft-spoken and kind. "You're among friends, Steven. We understand you."

"Bullshit!" Drak spat, again recoiling and attempting to kick out at anyone within his reach. "You're all full of bullshit. You're all maniacs," Drak screamed to no one in particular.

A brilliant light was directed in his face, its beam blinding Drak to all that was around him.

"My name is Dr. Morse. My specialty is the study of scanners," came a voice from beyond the light.

"Scanners? What the hell are scanners?" Drak asked, more uncertain of his fate now than ever.

"That's what you are, Steve," continued Dr. Morse. "A scanner. A very special person with very special talents which we would like to study."

"You are maniacs," was Drak's response after several seconds of silence. "A 'scanner' huh? They called me a lot of things in the nuthouse, but never a 'scanner.' "

"Those people didn't understand," added Morse, moving now in front of the light so that his body was silhouetted in its strong beam. "They thought you were sick, but we know better. We know you're not sick, Steven. We know you're not crazy either. Try to understand me. You are a very unique person with a very unique kind of power. So special, in fact, that our police commander over here needs your help. Can you help us, Steven?"

The room went quiet as Drak considered the concept of being a very special person with unusual talents. Someone so wonderful that the police—the fucking cops, for crying out loud—expected him to help them. Hah. Obviously, some kind of trap, Drak thought suspiciously.

"I don't believe you," he finally said. "What could you possibly want with me?"

Morse kept up his calm reassurance. "We won't send you back to the hospital, I promise you that. We will treat you like a very, very special guest here in our home."

Drak couldn't believe his ears. Just how stupid did these creeps think he was. Their home. It was a fucking hospital, man. Glancing suspiciously at Forrester across the room and then back again at Morse, Drak quietly scanned into the doctor's mind with a twisted leer. Sensing the invasion, Morse quietly moved back into the light, but not fast enough. Drak had sucked the truth from Morse's thoughts.

"You'll do something worse!" Drak screamed. "Stick wires in my head. Try to control me like maniacs. Well, it won't work, you hear me. *IT WON'T WORK*!"

Drak struggled to free himself from his bonds, to escape the penetrating light that was frying his very skull. He wailed with frustrated rage and anger but the straps holding his arms to the chair held firm.

"The wires aren't to control you," Morse shouted to get his attention. Then quietly he added, "They're to help. I want you to help me, and at the same time I'll help you, Steven."

Drak watched as the doctor walked slowly past the light and around the chair. Morse continued to speak in a patronizing voice, much like baby-sitters do when trying to coerce a child into an early bed. When the doctor finally came full circle and stood in front of Drak, the scanner seized his opportunity.

With an intensity which even surprised him, Drak scanned Morse with such force that the doctor lost his balance and fell backward across the room. Morse was already rolling on the floor, desperately trying to escape, but Drak was merciless in his attack. Again he scanned, again he saw the doctor coil up in pain.

"Let me outta here!" Drak screamed as he moved his attention around the room.

It took Feck longer than it should have to realize that Drak was not kidding. He cocked his tranquilizer gun and quickly rushed in front of Drak for a clear shot at his chest.

It was a move only an idiot would have attempted, and Feck fit the bill.

Drak first scanned the rifle out of Feck's hand, and than scanned his would-be attacker back across the room. Feck hit the lab table with such force that its metal legs buckled, sending equipment crashing to the ground. Syringe needles rolled across the floor and as Feck tried to stand, he lost his footing again, this time without Drak's help.

On the sidelines, Forrester was actually beginning to enjoy the destruction around him. It had all the elements of a dime-store novel, and the large amount of physical pain satisfied his sadistic temperament.

From the floor, Dr. Morse screamed for mercy. "Help me. Forrester. Feck. EPH-2. Hurry!"

"No wait, wait . . ." Forrester tried to intervene, hoping to delay the inevitable.

But Forrester was too late. Feck had already picked up an EPH-2 syringe from the floor and before Drak could react, he stabbed it deep into the scanner's neck. It was only seconds before the EPH-2 began to work on Drak's rage. First came the characteristic uncontrollable weeping; then, a rush of euphoric laughter; finally, sleep.

As Feck removed Drak's restraints, the scanner collapsed to the floor in a drugged heap. Not missing an opportunity, Feck kicked him hard in the ribs.

"You sonofabitch," he muttered under his breath, slamming the toe of his workboots deep into Drak's side before grabbing him by his feet and pulling him out of the room.

Forrester was furious. It had all ended so fast. So wrong.

"It was the only way," Morse responded before Forrester could even speak.

"Now we'll never know, will we?" the police commander asked, his face full of rage. "Drak was a perfectly potent scanner, but you're going to turn him into another of your EPH-2 junkies, Morse. What a waste. What a goddamn waste."

Dr. Morse ignored the put-down, preferring instead to concentrate on putting his lab table back in place and assessing the damage to the room.

"He'll want more now, you know. They all want more. And then more. And then more. It just doesn't stop, does it? You can't make it stop," Forrester blurted out, openly hostile. "Within six months, he'll start to degenerate. Within a year, he'll be worthless."

As Morse and Forrester left the lab and began the long walk down the darkened hallway, the doctor began to question whether the police commander was partially right. He knew his experiments had their problems—just as he knew that one day he would find the right dosage of EPH-2 that would make scanners controllable.

Midway down the corridor, the men paused outside a viewing window of a larger cell. The sight inside was disgusting, even for those who had witnessed it often.

Five men and women were inside, all degenerating scanners—once healthy human beings now wasting away under the influence of EPH-2 addiction. The oldest looked worst, of course; he had the graying, hollow look of cancer patients nearing the end. Wasting away, yet craving the very chemical that was destroying them from the inside.

"This is pathetic," Forrester could only comment. In this room, EPH-2 was freely available. Patients shared needles. It mattered little what other disease they might be spreading. Their addiction would kill them long before any virus or bacteria would have a chance. They were saucereyed, mumbling basket-cases, doomed to a painful and tragic death.

"It's the only way to control them," Morse answered his critic. "It's the only way we can keep them from hurting us and everyone else, don't you see. Besides, I think Drak is strong enough that with a new combination of EPH-2 and some psychotropics I've been working on, we could get some miles out of him."

Forrester remained unconvinced. He just watched silently in horror at the sight before him.

David's dorm room needed a personal touch. True, there were the necessary items, a twin bed, a worn desk, a small bookshelf, and the tiniest of closets, but there were none of the other typical touches of a college student. There were no posters hanging on the walls; no photographs from home or from a special girl; not even dirty clothes thrown in the corner waiting for wash day.

It was the kind of place that looked barely lived in. Less a home away from home than a place to shower, change, and be gone in a flash. Perhaps the noise level made it seem more brash. The sound of rock music blared from the room next door as David stood checking out his reflection in the mirror, telephone in hand.

His body had the look of a natural athlete—tight, sinewy, with thighs thick from farm labor. His shoulders were broad and covered with freckles, as much a sign of long hours of work in the sun as of heritage.

He liked what he saw as he flexed his arms and danced in place to the constant bass beat from next door.

"What? I can't hear you?" he yelled into the telephone receiver. "No. How *could* it be serious, Mother? It's our first date, for crying out loud. I don't even know if it *is* a date, really. It was all her idea!"

Cupping the receiver to his chin, David pulled on a

pair of jeans, worn in just the right spots and to the right shade. They wrapped his legs with innocent seduction.

"Yeah, school's fine, Dad. It's great. I still haven't met too many people, but I like it here . . ."

The sound of banging on his door interrupted his sentence and the call.

"I've got to go. I'll call you tomorrow, okay? Bye."

Hanging up quickly, David moved to the door. The music from the next room seemed to be getting louder and louder, a sign of another headache beginning, and he wiped at his brow.

His hand grabbed at the knob, unsure whether to open the door. The persistence of the knock made the decision.

Snapping out of his daze, David opened his dorm room door a few inches. Alice was standing with her back to him now, dancing silently in the hallway. She was surprised when he spoke in barely audible tones, a frog catching in his throat.

"You're early," he said, feeling ridiculous hiding partially behind his door.

"You'd be surprised what you find when you show up early, David," Alice smiled, turning toward him and pushing her way into the room. "Why, David Ketchum, you're quite a hunk," she said, eyeing his bare chest with obvious appreciation.

More embarrassed now than ever, David quickly reached in his closet for a shirt, fully aware that Alice continued to check out his body.

Dressed in a sexy black outfit, Alice was quite impressive herself. The clingy, perfectly tailored dress sent a message that David read loud and clear. Alice's city-sophisticated good looks were more striking now than ever, he mused. He felt his face blazing to a blush as she caught him watching her move across the room. Finally he managed to get his arm in his jacket and flip up the collar.

"Ready to roll," she said, raising her left eyebrow the way David had seen some actresses do on television.

Yup, he decided, this was definitely a date.

The drive to the indoor mall went all too quickly as David found himself drawn to the kindness of his first friend in town. It was her suggestion to try a new Italian place—Chao Bambino. The food was both plentiful and delicious.

David couldn't help staring into Alice's eyes as she spoke of her hometown and the many friends she had left behind to attend veterinarian college. He found it comforting to ask the questions instead of answering them.

By the time he finished his ravioli with a side order of mozzarella marinara, David had learned that Alice was one of three children (two older brothers were both studying to be attorneys), that her mother had died two years ago from an aneurysm, and that her favorite sport was tennis, though she hadn't played it in years.

"One thing about the city, they feed you well," Alice laughed as she tried to adjust her dress around an inflated stomach.

"But you pay for it," David added, then wished he had kept his mouth shut, hoping she didn't notice how he carefully added up the check twice and then took his time calculating the tip.

Walking out of the restaurant, Alice was still smiling as she turned away from several lovely dresses in a trendy boutique's window and paused on the corner to look David straight in the face.

"Why did you decide to leave home and come here to vet school?" she asked.

"What I know about most is taking care of animals.

I know how they feel inside. I've always known," he said, trying to sound sincere without seeming like a farm hand.

Alice couldn't help but notice the anxiety in David's eyes as he struggled to divert her attention by putting his arm around her shoulder.

"Is something wrong, David," she asked, turning toward him again. "Is it those headaches?"

"Yeah," he said lying, yet relieved that she found an excuse for his awkwardness.

"You know what's good for a headache, don't you?" Alice asked, drawing herself closer to David's chest. Lightly touching the sides of his head, she slowly massaged his temples with her fingertips and gently, ever so innocently, kissed him on the lips.

Their mouths touched moistly as David returned her embrace, happy she had made it easy for him. Happy she had made the first move.

"You are a doctor, aren't you," he finally said when their lips parted.

Alice loved the effect she had on this guy, loved the way he reacted to her teasing. "Well, I do have my way with humans," she answered, eyes twinkling in the cool night air.

"Did you ever try this," David countered, lifting her up to reach his lips and holding her in a tight embrace.

Gasping for breath, Alice had to admit that midair embraces were a first. "And I thought you were shy," she laughed.

"Only around humans," David answered in an odd tone of voice.

"And what am I?" Alice joked.

"I'm not sure," David teased. "Let me take another look." And with that the pair entwined their bodies and began to kiss in earnest. The footsteps of passing strangers did little to interrupt their moment of passion, and only after a small eternity did the pair pause, unsure of where their desires might lead.

David was in paradise. The scent of Alice's perfume was driving him crazy; months of bridled emotion begged to be released. As he reached for Alice's waist to wrap her in still another embrace, she took his hand and pulled him reluctantly down the street.

"Come on, big boy," she teased. "Let's cool you down with a little beer."

The idea of going into a crowded bar was not David's concept of fun. He wanted to say no, to tell her he knew how he would react. But she seemed to be having such a good time that any thought of disappointing her was out of the question.

Pushing past the doorman who looked like he recognized Alice from previous visits, the pair entered the trendy upscale cocktail lounge. The darkness of the place took some getting used to, its mirrored ceiling balls reflecting beams of subtle light into the corners and onto the dance floor. Smoke seemed to be everywhere, dancing in wisps above candlelit tables, settling on the ceiling like a cloud of nicotine.

A band called X-TRA was just finishing their current set, relying as much on noise as on talent in performing their music. The crowd on the dance floor matched those standing around in loose pairs—chic, well-groomed, and expensively dressed.

As David was pulled to the bar through the tightly packed room, a few strangers turned to shout their hellos to Alice, while smiling at him in silent introduction. The noise was building in his head, and David's face began to reflect just how uncomfortable it was beginning to make him feel. Surely Alice could see what was happening; perhaps she would suggest they leave.

"Wait here while I find us two beers," was her only comment as David looked pleadingly in her direction.

The push of bodies against his seemed to be coming from all sides as David tried to maneuver to a neutral corner. But there was no escaping the constant beat of the band, which had begun to play a synthesized version of Stravinsky's *Fire Bird Suite*. It was a loud invasion into his senses turning his mind into stricken confusion.

Voices began to echo inside his head as every sound, every movement, was magnified a hundredfold. David tried to stop the assault, covering his ears. Yet, onward they came, unrelenting.

As the pressure built inside his head, David felt the blood pumping madly through his body. Beads of perspiration began to run down his forehead and he grabbed for the edge of the bar in support. Gasping for air and out of control, David staggered past Alice and aimed for the door.

Putting down the beers, Alice pushed past the crowds of onlookers, unable to reach David before he collapsed by the door.

"David!" she screamed as the doorman cleared the area, assuming he was dealing with another typical drunk.

"Look, young lady," he turned to Alice. "Your friend should sleep this one off. You want help to your car?" he asked sincerely.

"He's sick, not drunk," she screamed hysterically, bending to help David to a nearby chair.

"It's okay. It's okay," David panted, barely audible above the band. "I gotta get some air," he said as he lunged past the doorman out into the street.

Catching up to him, Alice was concerned and shocked, placing her arm around his shoulder.

He felt like a child being mothered. Yet, right now, that's what he needed. "These migraines. I've been getting so many of them lately," he said. Looking up at her worried expression, he added, "I'm sorry. I was having a good time. Really."

Unconvinced, Alice motioned toward his truck. "I'm taking you home."

"No, no. I'm okay," David insisted. "I'm okay. I'll be fine, you'll see."

Unrelenting, Alice took his arm gently. As they stepped off the curb, a young kid on a BMX bike zigzagged across their path. Showing off to all who would watch, he popped a wheelie and spun 360 degrees on his rear wheel.

"Hey," Alice yelled, to no avail. The youngster's walkman was blaring rock music into his ears and he had little time for casual reprimands.

Out of nowhere a car turned the corner, speeding in the kid's direction. Too fast, David thought. Too fast on this narrow street.

Totally unaware of impending doom, the boy aimed his bike toward the center of the street in preparation for another stunt. Only then did he see the oncoming car. Trying to brake but unable to stop, the boy slid off his bike, landing directly in the path of the approaching auto.

Without thinking, David scanned his eyes in the driver's direction. David made contact with the teenager behind the wheel, commanding him to stop without saying a word. It seemed the driver involuntarily slammed on his brakes, turning the wheel in obvious panic.

As the car screeched to a halt just inches from the boy's head, the street filled with bystanders amazed at what had just happened. Rising slowly to his feet, the youngster was obviously in shock, speechless from the experience. So, too, was the driver, who continued to stare in disturbed amazement.

Jumping from his car and shaking from shock, the guy choked out, "Jesus, I didn't even see him."

Only Alice really understood what he was saying. As she stared back at David in disbelief, shuddering involuntarily, his gaze still fixed on the steering wheel.

CHAPTER THREE

THE NEW ORDER

The following news report appeared nationally via World Press International. Its headline read:

LAWLESSNESS AT ALL-TIME HIGH
By Donald Sanders
Staff Writer

A recent study prepared by the Center for Criminal Control in Washington, D.C., that surveyed 100 metropolitan areas in the United States, revealed frightening statistics suggesting that crime in this country has reached an all-time high.

According to the report, prepared in conjunction with local law enforcement organizations, murder has increased a shocking 16 percent in the past two years alone—second only to armed robbery, up 22 percent in the same time-period.

Burglary and rape are also on the rise—both up 8 percent in the past twenty-four months—with kidnapping escalating at an alarming 6 percent since the last study was taken. Even more disturbing is the fact that each of the dozen crimes tallied in the report showed increases in frequency over the past two years.

Justice Department head Alexander Conover is understood to have briefed the White House on the contents of the study before it was released yesterday. Pressured by such staggering increases in lawlessness in the nation's cities, the President is said to be planning to divert more funding to crime prevention in his annual budget due before Congress in less than a month's time.

Testifying before the House Committee on Lawlessness in the United States, special presidential advisor Dr. Valerie Reynolds pointed to overcrowded jails and correctional facilities as only part of the problem. She stated that law enforcement officials in this country have had their hands tied for too long by regulations which are both outdated and restrictive. "It is time that we enlisted the aid of our neighbors and friends to assist our police in apprehending and convicting these criminals whose acts violate the rights of every law-abiding citizen in this country," Reynolds said in a speech which lasted well past her allotted fifteen-minute limit.

In a press conference on the steps of the Capitol, Conover dismissed Reynold's charges as "radical" and "outside the fundamental guidelines established by the President." When questioned by reporters on expected ac-

*tion from the White House, Conover said that the President
is expected to address the issue personally in a White House
press conference next week.*

*What can't be ignored, however, are the shocking sta-
tistics that continue to echo throughout Washington, D.C.
The enormity of the problem is such that immediate action
on a national level is needed, with all branches of the federal
government expected to join together in formulating a plan
for positive action.*

The flushing of a toilet meant they were not alone. Feck
and Gruner walked silently up to the row of marble sinks
in the elegant men's room on the seventh floor of the Armstrong Building, pretending to comb their hair. Well, Feck
combed his hair; Gruner was already so bald that any attempt
to move around the few remaining strands would only have
lead to laughter.

They needed a fix and they needed it bad. The effect
of their last dose of EPH-2 was wearing off, and both men
knew that the syringes in their pocket were their only sal-
vation.

An elderly man slowly exited the third stall from the
end and shuffled his way to join Feck at the sinks. Watching
him reach down and wash his hands was like watching a
movie in slow motion.

Come on, already, old man, Feck thought, resisting
the urge to scan him right out the door.

With an equal lack of speed, the old-timer excused
himself as he moved tentatively past Gruner to the paper-
towel holder hanging nearby. Losing his patience, Gruner
grabbed a handful of towels and shoved them at the man
with such force that the kindly looking gray-haired codger
stopped in his tracks, frozen in fear.

"Kinda slow, ain't you, pops," Gruner sneered in his

most polite manner. And with that, he gently but firmly started to push the intruder toward the men's room exit.

Feck couldn't wait until the guy hit the hallway. Already he was rolling up his sleeve, his eyes glazed, preparing to inject himself with the life-giving serum. Gruner was right behind him, copying his every move.

In their rush to get a fix, neither man even bothered to wipe their arms with alcohol and disinfect the syringe. There was only one thing on their minds—the craving they both were feeling with such intensity that they would have gladly killed to satisfy their need.

Feck was first to feel the rush of the EPH-2 high. The routine was familiar to them both. Tears began to flood from Feck's eyes, and sobbing tore through his soul. The familiar depression that fermented within his mind was only temporary. By the time Gruner began to cry, Feck was already laughing. Step two in the mood swings toward stability.

By the time they both tossed their syringes in the trash bin and checked their expensive suits in the mirror, a good twenty minutes had passed. Twenty minutes that would mean death to some.

Karman Lucret was sitting behind his desk in his expensively decorated office when the buzz came over the intercom. The modern art decorating his walls would have been more at home in a museum, such was its quality and worth. The power of the man was in evidence everywhere, from his marble-topped desk to the diamonds on his fingers.

"I told you to leave the judge to me," Lucret repeated into the telephone. "You're trying my patience. Five-hundred K," he said, raising his voice now. "Have it delivered in cash, and I'll have you out in forty-eight hours. Be cool, man," he said, rolling his eyes and hanging up the receiver.

Rising from his desk, the heavyset man rotated his

neck in an attempt to rid himself of obvious tension. The cost of power was evident in his physical condition: overweight, gray circles under his eyes, a rasp in his labored breathing. He lit up a cigar as he hit the button on his intercom with a heavily ringed finger. "Send in the 'gentlemen' from Palm Beach," he directed in a mocking voice.

Lucret returned to his highback leather chair and turned his back to the office door, gazing instead at the Monet hanging behind his desk.

As Feck and Gruner entered, he didn't bother to get up. He didn't even turn to face them immediately. Lucret's bullet-head bodyguard, a South American named Palomino, gestured toward the unpadded chairs in front of the desk. Only after Feck and Gruner approached the chairs did Lucret speak, instinctively knowing where they were.

"Misters Feck and Gruner . . . Sit," he commanded, spinning in his chair, sending cigar smoke trailing like a skywriter.

"Pleased to meet you, Mr. Lucret," Feck forced himself to say, holding out his hand in greeting.

Ignoring any attempted handshake, Lucret sized up the strangers before him. "From Palm Beach, huh?" he repeated what he had been told.

"That's right," Feck answered, unsure of his ground and wishing Gruner would stop making strange smacking sounds with his lips. "Mr. Montoya told us you were the price of doing business in his town."

Lucret didn't like it. He didn't like the looks of these two jerks, and he didn't like their smell. He had been a lawyer far too long to be taken in by amateurs like these. Ugly amateurs at that. "So, how can I help you, gentlemen?" he asked, knowing that whatever these jokers would say would be a lie.

"We've got a pipeline for fifty keys a month, right from Peru. Only this ain't our turf. We need introductions," Feck said, getting right to specifics.

It was a little too fast, and a little too pat for Lucret. He bristled at the idea of talking about drug running with strangers and didn't like it one bit that they thought he could provide them safe passage in his town. He was done playing with these clowns. He was no longer amused.

"By the way, your introduction, Mr. Montoya," Lucret said, staring directly at Feck. "He happens to have been cremated two weeks ago. And, you two look about as suntanned as calamari."

Feck and Gruner stiffened with the news.

Rising from his chair, cigar pointed straight forward, Lucret turned cold. No one tried to move into his territory, especially not two brainless nobodies. "Who the hell do you think you're fucking with here?" he cracked, crushing his cigar in the crystal ashtray on his desk. "I am the best lawyer in this town; the best insurance policy money can buy."

Outside the Armstrong Building, in a dark and lonely side street, the radio in Forrester's Buick was picking up the bugged conversation clearly. "I am the best lawyer in this town; the best insurance policy money can buy," came across the receiver.

Forrester greeted the news with a laugh. "Not any-more, Karman baby," he chuckled. "Not anymore."

It was what he had waited all night to hear. He had gone through a family bucket of Kentucky Fried Chicken and had nearly frozen to death in the dark alley waiting for Feck and Gruner to get this far. Now, they only had to finish their business and he could call it a night.

* * *

Palomino was on alert and Lucret snapped his fingers, sitting back down in his chair. "Show these zombies the stairs. Adios, gentlemen," he said, stretching out the syllables on the last word in disdain.

As Palomino reached for his .45, Gruner sprung into action, scanning him in one swift move. Palomino was thrown back across the room. He crashed headlong into a brass sculpture which toppled off its marble pedestal onto him.

Too late, Lucret tried to telephone for help. Feck's scan was too strong, too quick, for the fat, tired lawyer. The force of Feck's scan froze Lucret's hand to the phone and he started shaking. First slowly, then with increasing intensity, the attorney sizzled as an electrical force fried through his body.

As Feck increased the intensity of his scan, Lucret was smashed against the back wall, the Monet falling to the floor, its frame and glass smashing. It was only as he gasped for breath and clutched desperately at his temples that Lucret felt the first trickle of blood from his ears and nostrils.

"Little nosebleed, Lucret? Better go easy on the blow, counselor," Feck laughed mockingly.

Pointing to the wall safe that the Monet had once concealed, Feck continued to increase the intensity of the scan until Lucret was forced to move over to the combination lock. Hoping that the pair would be satisfied with its contents, Lucret spun the dial—first right, then left, then right again. The safe didn't open. Haste made waste.

Again he tried, again he failed. "Damn it," he moaned, aware that the pressure from Feck's scan was controlling his mind and preventing him from concentrating. Finally, the combination clicked into place, and Lucret opened the safe door with his blood-covered hand.

Several kilos of cocaine and bundles of cash were hidden behind a camouflage of legal papers and notes. Pushing Lucret roughly aside, Feck pulled apart the contents and began to neatly arrange the drugs and money across the desktop.

Gruner couldn't help but grin. This was too easy. Yet, he knew his fun was only starting. "Up and at 'em," he said to Palomino, still lying dazed on the floor. "This is your big scene."

The South American palooka groaned as he tried to move the heavy statue off his chest. Against his will, he was forced to his feet, Gruner commanding his every move with the force of his scan.

Visibly trembling, Palomino slowly raised his .45 straight in front of him. His arms were being controlled for him; his finger was forced to press against the trigger. Horrified, and screaming in anticipation of what he was about to do, Palomino aimed at his friend Lucret, pulling the trigger once, twice, three times.

"No loyalty. No loyalty at all," Gruner punned, as Lucret's ripped body fell to the floor with a bloody thud.

With Gruner momentarily distracted, Palomino was freed from his mind and his grasp. Retreating out of self-preservation, Palomino charged through the office door toward the reception area beyond.

Forrester, Gelson, and two young cops were already positioned as he burst through the door into the empty office lobby. Their weapons drawn, they wasted no time as Palomino sprinted toward the elevator.

"Freeze!" Forrester yelled, a matter of procedure more than instruction.

Without waiting for Palomino to drop his weapon, the two cops opened fire, hitting the South American and splattering the office area with his blood. He was dead before he hit the floor.

Forrester couldn't help the urge to kick the dead body, watching as blood continued to drain from the multiple wounds.

"Another successful police operation," he snickered in Gelson's direction. Neither man noticed as Feck and Gruner slipped away, unaware of the cocaine residue still on their noses.

It would be only a matter of minutes before the television news crews would arrive, Forrester knew. He took the time to remove syringes from the men's room and wash his face. The camera had a way of making him look older, washing out his complexion after a long day.

The officers were instructed to cooperate fully with the cameramen as they hastily set up their sun-guns, microphones, and other equipment. Palomino's body was left on full display as an example of what Forrester knew would mean action in the mayor's office.

As paramedics struggled to carry out the remains of Lucret on a stretcher, Forrester lead two news crews into the decimated office. Cash and cocaine were still stacked on the desk; blood was smeared across the wall; broken glass and furniture set the stage.

"Commander Forrester," questioned top news reporter Carole White, "could you explain what happened here?"

Could he explain? Of course, he could explain, he thought to himself. She hadn't asked for the truth, just an explanation, after all.

Waiting a beat to make certain that the camera was in focus, Forrester directed his appeal to the shocked viewers at home. "This office belongs, used to belong, to Karman Lucret, the most corrupt lawyer in the city. He took criminals out of jail and put them back on the street. Now he doesn't," Forrester said bluntly. The cameraman zoomed in for a close-up as Forrester pursed his lips and dramatically steeled his jaw.

In his dorm room, David Ketchum was doing his sit-ups and watching TV. He paused to turn up the volume when he recognized the police commander.

"It's about time that the citizens of this city, and the entire nation, realize something," Forrester was saying. "Crime is no longer an activity that occurs only on the margins of society. It occurs at its heart. It has invaded its vital organs. It infects business leaders, politicians, lawyers, doctors," Forrester said, poignantly adding "policeman" as the last on the list.

Back in Lucret's office, the heat of the lamps was causing beads of perspiration to drain across Forrester's upper lip. He was driving home a message that he had rehearsed many times before in the privacy of his bedroom, echoing his comments to his mirror in solitary dictation. Now the entire city, perhaps the entire country, would hear his plan.

"If we are going to save the society, we're going to have to cure crime," he stressed, looking directly into the camera lens. "To cure it, we'll need new and more powerful medicines. We'll need 'surgical procedures' like the one you saw here tonight. And we're going to need surgeons."

Forrester felt the strength of his speech in his body. He needed this moment to launch his political career. It was his destiny. Slowly, with calm intelligence and articulation, he began to reveal what had to be told. Unpleasant truths that could no longer be denied. The voice of reason in a time of turmoil.

"Surgeons who are not afraid to replace the flaccid public officials of our government who have permitted and, yes, even encouraged, this disease," Forrester said, gesturing toward the desktop covered in cocaine. "We need an entire new order in our society. A coalition of political figures and law enforcement officers and decent citizens like yourselves."

The die had been cast. Forrester knew he was right.

Police Commissioner Mitchell Stokes didn't agree. He was large. A bull of a man. And when Stokes came charging into a room, people tended to listen.

He was the kind of guy who didn't like surprises and rarely got them. Tonight was an exception. As he lay in bed watching the eleven o'clock news, he was shocked to hear about the shooting death of Lucret and Palomino. Anytime a police officer fired his weapon and killed a suspect it concerned him. But nothing in his thirty-two years on the force had prepared him for Forrester's monologue. He was stunned by what sounded like public disapproval of his administration and that of the mayor's. And he was not alone.

No sooner had the telecast finished then Stokes's phone began to ring. The mayor wanted to see him, and see him now! He expected the worst. And he got it.

The next morning, Forrester was walking on air. So pleased with himself that he was even speaking nicely to his nosy neighbor, Mrs. Katz, a miracle in itself. By the time he had reached his downtown office, he had been recognized at least a dozen times, and only one person had something nasty to vent.

Forrester's smile stretched ear to ear. And it was that smile which first caught Stokes's attention as he stormed into Forrester's office, wanting some answers and expecting to get them.

"Oh, hello, Commissioner," Forrester said cheerily as he hung up the telephone after speaking with his tailor. Public figures should maintain their appearance and Forrester knew he needed several new suits.

"Wipe that ridiculous smile off your face," Stokes boomed in a voice that could be heard into the elevator lobby. "Just who do you think you are talking to the press like that without my authorization?" he demanded, slamming his fist down on Forrester's desk scattering papers to the floor.

"I was a bit overzealous, perhaps, Commissioner," Forrester said, in a facetious tone. "I apologize," he added as an afterthought.

Stokes was not to be placated so easily. This time, Forrester had gone too far. Overzealous indeed. For the past six years, his police chief had been running the department just barely skirting scandal and investigation. Now Stokes himself had been held up to public humiliation. Overzealous, bullshit!

"Apologize to the mayor. She's had smoke coming out of her ears all night over your 'flaccid public officials' line. And so have I." He paused to stare Forrester into submission. It was all he could do to keep from cracking him right across his smirking face. "And what the hell is this 'new order' of yours?" he asked, still piercing the chief with his gaze.

"Just rhetoric, Commissioner. Mere rhetoric," Forrester gleamed.

"You're a fucking idiot. The only 'new order' around here is going to be after I investigate your 'special unit'. With that, Stokes stormed out as he entered, in a fury, slamming the door behind him.

"Have a nice day," Forrester murmured to himself, the ear-to-ear grin back in place.

* * *

There was a stillness in the night as Forrester rounded the bend and made his way up the long driveway leading to the Neurological Research Institute, the official name given to Morse's lab. The starkness of the windowless facility made Forrester shiver unconsciously, knowing full well the evil that went on behind its high stone walls.

Pulling his car across the bridge that led to the guarded institute gate, Forrester couldn't help but feel that he was alone in his fight for a "clean" society. One in which law and order was omnipotent. One in which the scum of this planet was eradicated.

As the security guard watched, Forrester punched in a private code at the gate, and waited patiently as it slowly opened electronically. Forrester parked in front of the main building and walked quickly to the entrance, suddenly aware of the damp cold night air.

"You said the commissioner wouldn't be a problem," Dr. Morse said as he met Forrester at the door.

"I told you he won't be, and he won't," Forrester snapped back, not needing more criticism—especially not from Dr. Morse.

As Morse began to argue, the sudden sounding of a piercing alarm jolted him into action.

"Shit!" was the only word he uttered as he turned to run down the long hallway ahead. With Forrester close at his heels, he skipped the elevator and ran into the stairwell, vaulting down two steps at a time in the rush to the basement level.

Morse and Forrester hit the hallway running toward the red blinking light that signaled the source of the trouble. It was the large padded holding room containing the five degenerate scanners. In one corner, an orderly had corralled four of the scanners, who were in shock and quivering at the sight before them.

The youngest female scanner was convulsing on the floor, while another orderly attempted to keep her in place. "She's in terminal phase, Doctor," the orderly explained unnecessarily. Unfortunately, they had seen this scenario played out far too often. They knew there was nothing that could be done.

Seeing Dr. Morse approach, the female scanner became even more hysterical, wanting to be put out of her misery. "Just kill me," she screamed, as her legs and arms continued to jerk violently. "Please, kill me. Christ! The pressure."

Morse snapped his fingers at the orderly for a syringe of EPH-2, knowing in his heart it was a useless effort. He needn't have bothered. Before the orderly could move at his command, the woman convulsed one last time. As the blood began to pour from her ears and nose, not even Forrester could watch the sight.

As he left the room, Forrester seemed emotionally moved at the young scanner's death. Dr. Morse followed him down the corridor, wondering at the police officer's uncharacteristic display of grief.

"I knew that girl," the policeman finally volunteered. "I knew her from the old neighborhood. She was always so shy, so withdrawn. No one should have to end life like that."

Morse was almost touched by Forrester's unusual suggestion of sympathy. It didn't last long.

"Another one gone. This just isn't working, Morse," was his comment by the time they reached the doctor's office. "You're losing too many, too fast."

Morse understood exactly what Forrester meant. The

supply of scanners was at an all-time low. Thinking out loud, he agreed. "The only functional scanners we have left are Feck, Gruner, and Drak."

"Drak? You call *that* functional?" Forrester shot back, pointing up to the TV monitor on the wall.

Drak was visible, crouching in the corner of another room, almost out of camera range.

"He's got tremendous command over his powers," Morse argued. "He could bounce back."

Even as he was uttering the words, Drak was proving him wrong. Fumbling with a syringe of EPH-2, Drak was injecting himself for a third time that night. For a new scanner in the program, it was a tremendous dose. As the men watched the display of excess without speaking, Drak fell back in bed, grabbing the remote for his VCR. A slasher movie flashed onto the screen as he began to giggle uncontrollably.

Dr. Morse was obviously distraught, helped not a bit by Forrester's constant pressure to deliver. "What we need is a clean scanner. A virgin mind," he said as both men looked back at Drak on the screen.

David Ketchum was exceedingly happy for perhaps the first time in his life. He was in love, and he wanted the world to know. As he drove along a busy campus road, he had to keep himself from shouting the news out the window of his truck to passersby walking on the street. He felt like Gene Kelly in *Brigadoon*, about to burst into a chorus of "Almost Like Being in Love." All right, so he knew he watched too many old musicals, but what else did he have to do growing up alone all those years in Vermont.

Parking his truck on a side street, he was smiling widely as he pulled a little bundle, wrapped in a wool blanket, from the front seat of the cab. He held it close to his chest as he walked up to the front of an old Victorian-type house, badly in need of paint.

Inside, Alice was involved in a major challenge. She had offered to cook a meal for David, and now was finding herself panicking at the very concept. Perhaps she had been a bit hasty in suggesting he come for dinner, but, after all, how difficult could pasta with pesto sauce be, she thought.

Just as she heard his knock on the door, she answered her own question. The container of pesto sauce in the refrigerator—a special recipe sent through the mail by her father—had started to spawn some blue fuzzy-looking spots inside the lid of the jar.

"Damn," Alice said unexpectedly out loud.

"Hey, is that how you greet a hungry traveler bearing gifts," she heard David say through the door.

Smiling, she told him to come in as she quickly dumped the remaining pesto sauce into the garbage disposal. In mock annoyance, at the sight of David, she added, "Him. He always drops by when dinner's ready."

Laughing, David gave her a small kiss and the news. "This is a little surprise to make our first dinner at home complete."

Handing Alice the blanket and stepping back, David waited for what he knew was about to happen.

"Oh, my God!" Alice exclaimed as she saw a small puppy wiggle out from under the covers. It was the sick little dog from vet school, now licking her face in obvious joy.

"He's okay. He's completely cured," David announced proudly.

The look on Alice's face said it all. She was astonished. Surprised at the gift of a puppy; amazed at the impossible recovery this dog had made. "He's adorable," she had to admit.

"And he's yours," David added to make certain there was no misunderstanding. "What are you going to name him?" he asked, already having his favorite name in mind.

"Trooper," she said without hesitation. "Because he made it. Because he survived."

Gathering an old box from the corner of the kitchen and placing the blanket carefully inside, Alice prepared Trooper's new home, instantly taking to the idea of having a new friend in her life.

The sound of David's stomach growling brought her mind back to dinner. "By the way, David," she cooed, as she placed Trooper in the box, "we've had a little accident with the pesto sauce. How about coming with me to the store to try to save a dinner for a swell fella?"

One glance over at Trooper told him everything was all right in that department. The little puppy was already fast asleep, rolled in a tiny ball and snoring gently.

"The store it is, my lady," David said, bowing from the waist like a medieval knight.

Helping Alice on with her jacket, David caught the scent of her perfume, the wonderful fragrance that reminded him of their first night together. He placed his arm gently around her shoulder as they started to walk around down the short street to the corner convenience store.

The minimart was more than convenient. It was one of those special places that seemed to have everything—from apples to zippers and everything in between. Although Alice never really met the owners, a black couple who worked the register with their daughter, they knew her on a first-name basis and were always interested in how her studies were progressing.

Tonight, however, she didn't have time to talk, other than asking, "Where's the pesto sauce?"

The owner's daughter at the register directed Alice

toward the refrigerator case in the rear of the store, while David headed toward a side aisle and the pet-food department.

The bright fluorescent lights and the clean, well-organized shelves gave the place a cheery feel, David thought as he moved past the bagged snack food, almost stopping to pick up some cookies.

The magazine counter across the aisle was too much to resist, especially after David found a digest called *Psychic Phenomena—A Handbook of PSI Discoveries.*

Alice found the pesto sauce and loaded her cart with three containers. She turned toward the cashier and was almost up to the register when she remembered she had forgotten to pick up a carton of milk.

"I just have to get some milk. Nature's perfect food," she joked with the young girl at the register.

"Sorry, but we have no milk," the cashier said, pointing to the newspaper headline taped by the counter that read: "CHILDREN DIE OF MILK POISONING—TAMPERING SUSPECTED."

"What kind of sicko would stick strychnine in kids' milk," the teenager asked.

Alice shook her head in disgust. "I hope they catch the bastard," she said as she looked up and caught David's reflection in the security mirror.

Just as the cashier began ringing up Alice's order, the doors of the store burst open. Two desperate-looking men dressed in ragged clothes charged the register. One, his eyes red from lack of sleep or booze or both, pulled a chrome-plated pistol from his pocket and pointed it at the black cashier. The other, a shorter guy, hardly older than a teen, drew a sawed-off shotgun from beneath his grungy duster and leveled it at Alice's stomach.

"All right, everyone. Freeze. Or we'll blow your

fuckin' heads off,'' the tall one said.''Out with the cash, including the floor safe, NOW!''

Alice, without thinking, glanced back at the security mirror to check for David. He was nowhere in sight. As her assailant held the shotgun almost touching her waist, Alice studied his face. He was Mexican, or maybe Spanish, she thought. A greasy glow covered his skin and hair, which was thick and black and wavy like a Latin romantic. There the similarity ended.

He had a long pointed nose that gave his face a weasel-like appearance, and as he sneered suspiciously in her direction, she noticed that his teeth were blackened with decay. She shuddered involuntarily at his disgusting presence and the power he had over her.

Grabbing Alice's purse, the man shoved her hard into the checkout counter, knocking a display of Lifesavers rolling across the floor. She hesitated to move a muscle, so erratic was his behavior.

Where is David? she couldn't help but wonder. Hoping that he was safely hidden, Alice once again stole a glance in the security mirror, seeing nothing but an empty aisle.

Actually David was anywhere but safe. As the action continued to center in the front of the store, David was maneuvering around back. Without a plan or weapon, he felt helpless to protect himself or Alice.

It didn't take long for disaster to strike. As the young cashier was filling several paper bags with money, she foolishly tried to trip the silent alarm. She would have done it, too, if it hadn't been for the Mexican's impatience.

Just as she was about to hit the button, he diverted his attention from Alice toward the register and saw her hand underneath the counter. Perhaps he thought she was trying to pull out a gun; perhaps he was just totally insane. At any rate, without a word, he blasted the girl point-blank in the chest. The impact hurled her body back into the rack of cigarettes behind her, killing her instantly.

Alice was splattered in blood; she began to scream hysterically. Now it was the tall punk's turn to become nervous.

"Shut up, bitch," he screamed, "or we'll do you, too."

Hearing the blast from his rear office, the cashier's father burst from the back of the store, shotgun in hand. If he had fired, he would have shot Alice for certain since the men had now positioned themselves behind her.

Before she could react, Alice was grabbed by both men, the taller one putting his pistol to her head. It was the opportunity the Mexican needed as he saw the owner divert his eyes for a moment. In that instant, he unloaded both his barrels into the man's chest, sending him slamming into the glass front of the beer cooler directly behind David.

"We're outta here!" the shorter guy shouted, grabbing the brown bag stuff with cash and heading toward the door.

"Let her go!" David shouted from his position in the rear of the store. Shocked that anyone else had witnessed their killings, the pair hesitated just long enough for David to act.

Scanning the Mexican with his eyes blazing, David sent the junkie crashing into a display of canned goods near the exit. Containers of Hawaiian pineapple rolled across the floor as the toppled display crumbled around the unconscious thief, his hand still clutching the bag of money.

"Crazy mother," the remaining partner shouted as he tried to vault over the counter for cover, firing wildly in David's direction.

Moving quickly now, David concentrated all his scanning power at the gunman's arm, lifting it straight up in the air even as the man continued to fire, unloading his pistol into the acoustical tile.

Not content with merely disarming him, David flipped the startled robber backward, and slid him through the pool of blood drained from the cashier's body. He rushed forward to help Alice and barely reached her as she fainted into his arms, bleeding from a head wound.

Outraged at the sight of her blood, David vented his anger again on the gunman, scanning him relentlessly as he attempted to regain his footing. Showing no mercy, harder and harder David concentrated his scan, almost enjoying the man's cries of pain.

"Aggh . . . no . . . no . . . STOP!" the tall, junkie screamed for compassion.

David relentlessly increased the power of his scan-tone until it reached an ear-wrenching squeal. The robber was paralyzed in his cramped stance, his spinal cord ripping under the pressure. He writhed in the trap of the scanner's power as the deadly force moved slowly, ever slowly, toward his head.

Caught in the strength of his own power, David turned up the intensity of his scan once more. The gunman had nowhere to run; no savior in sight. His head began to swell as the veins on the sides of his temple turned blue and swollen. Screaming his final sound of life, David watched with a fascinated gleam in his eyes as the scan turned the gunman's entire body into an electrical force, sending visible sparks of energy into the air.

David sent one final blast and the man's body rippled violently. In one swift moment, the entire back of his head exploded, sending blood and gray brain matter splashing across the register. Only then did David realize what he had done; only then did the full impact of his actions touch his heart.

Moving as much in shock as in terror, David bent down to cradle Alice's head in his arms; a security camera in the corner continuing to tape his every move.

Several days later, Police Commander Wayne Forrester would supply a copy of that tape to Dr. Gareth Morse. Over and over they would watch the destruction take place, freezing the frame at the moment when the tall robber's head exploded in a violent frenzy.

"You tell me," Forrester said, already knowing the answer.

"A beautiful, beautiful scanner," Morse replied. "I want him. And I want him now!"

CHAPTER FOUR

REVELATIONS

"For the past three weeks, this city has been stalked by fear," reported anchor Brian Nace on the late night newscast from WVTV-TV. "The now-notorious Milk Murderer struck again today, this time at the Eastside Elementary School where as many as sixteen children, all under the age of twelve, were poisoned by pint-containers of milk produced by the Fairchild Dairies.

"While none of the children died as a result of drinking the tainted milk, four remain in serious condition at Memorial Hospital this evening. To date, three deaths have been linked to consumption of Fairchild Dairy products.

Despite a voluntary recall of all milk products produced by the state's largest dairy processing plant, containers of milk deliberately laced with strychnine continue to turn up in the marketplace.

"The fourteen cartons of milk consumed at the Eastside School were part of a shipment which apparently had been placed weeks earlier in refrigerated storage units and only recently discovered. School officials said that they were investigating how recalled milk products could have been allowed into their cafeteria's current food chain.

"In the past three weeks, over four dozen cartons of milk have been discovered to have been tampered with, each containing enough poison to seriously injure an adult and most certainly kill most children. The largest quantity, some fifteen cartons, were pulled from a single convenience store on the South Side. In an effort to halt more poisonings, all major supermarket chains and most minimarkets have removed all milk products, including ice cream, from their shelves. Today's incident proves that this is still not enough.

"At a press conference hastily called at the Eastside School, Police Commander Wayne Forrester said that a special investigation unit had been formed to begin a concentrated effort to stop the poisonings from continuing. It is believed to be the work of a single mentally disturbed individual, although Forrester would give no additional information concerning any suspects in the crime. In the meantime, this city continues to be stalked by fear.

"For WVTV-TV, this is Brian Nace reporting."

It had been three days and three nights since the horror in the minimart. David replayed the incident over and over in his mind as he tried to understand what he had done and why.

Alice's condition was also foremost on his mind. She

had lost a great deal of blood from her head wound, and had actually lapsed into a coma for almost two days. As he sat in the plastic chair in the hospital waiting room, he had ample time to reflect on their short time together and how deeply he had grown to love her. He wanted desperately to see her and tell her in person. But so far her doctor refused to allow any visitors.

He was still in shock over the events of the past few days, and was concentrating so hard on the mystery of it all that he didn't even hear the approaching footsteps of a nurse coming toward him.

"Excuse me," she said, while nudging him politely back to the present. "You can see her now, but just for five minutes. She's still very weak."

Like a man with a renewed sense of being, David leapt from his chair and rushed down the hall, the nurse following slowly at a distance.

Reaching Alice's room, David paused to compose his thoughts. He felt his heart beating wildly inside his chest as he tried to gain the composure he needed to face Alice for the first time since the robbery.

Finally opening the door slowly, he entered the darkened room, fearing the worst. Alice looked gray and weak on the elevated bed before him. It broke his heart to see the assortment of tubes and wires connected to various parts of her body. Her head was wrapped entirely in bandages; her eyes blackened from the ordeal. The steady beep of the EKG machine stood in marked contrast to Alice's erratic labored breathing.

As he moved quietly to the side of her bed, and took her hand, she slowly opened her eyes and gazed deeply into his.

"David. What happened," she said, her voice thick with medication.

"It's all right. You're okay now. I'm here," he answered, feeling totally helpless.

"What about you?" she questioned, trying to turn to get a better look at him.

"I'm fine."

"But . . . in the store . . . what did you . . ."

David put his finger to her lips, silencing her for the moment. He didn't want her to recall the human devastation he had caused.

But Alice would not be silenced; her memory of that night was still vivid in her mind. "What happened to that man. I saw . . . that poor man."

David looked away, unable to bear the look in her eyes. Ashamed, awash in inner turmoil, he had no choice but to confess. "Ever since I was a little kid, I've been able to . . . well, to do things," he began, walking over to the window, and looking out into the hospital courtyard.

"David? What kind of things?" she asked, unable to focus completely across the room.

"Sort of telepathic things," he replied, turning to face her again. "Alice, I've never really understood it."

"The other night . . . you saved that boy on the bicycle, didn't you?"

Frustrated, confused, David walked back to the bed and reached for her hand. "I *had* to, so I did it. But it's never been like this. It's getting stronger and stronger. I can feel it welling up inside me. And I can't explain what's happening. Even more frightening," he paused and looked deeply into Alice's eyes, "I don't know how to stop it."

David could see the fear in his girlfriend's face. "This scares me," she said, reaching up to hug him.

"Me too, Alice. Me too."

He would have stayed all night if he could, but in several minutes—long minutes lost in silent pondering—

the nurse requested that David leave. The drive home was little more than a blur as the thought of his strange and frightening power occupied David's every thought.

By the time David walked slowly up the three flights of steps to his dormitory room, he was weary with apprehension. Feeling totally alone, totally without confidence, David wanted to escape this nightmare his life had become.

As he opened his door and turned on the lights, he was startled to be greeted by a stranger sitting on his bed.

"Hello, David. My name is Commander Forrester. I'm with the police," the serious-looking man said, attempting to put his mind at ease.

David recognized the police commander from his television appearance only days before. He also recognized danger in his voice. This man was not to be trusted, David felt in his heart.

"What . . . what do you want, and how did you get in here?" he demanded, trying to sound calm.

"You killed a man, son. You know that and I know that."

"I didn't touch the guy," David said, feeling his voice rise in his throat unintentionally.

"No, you didn't," Forrester countered. "That's what makes it so interesting, don't you think?"

David recoiled in fear. Backing toward the door, his mind was racing. His every thought was on escape; the alternative surely being prison.

Moving quickly to calm David, Forrester raised his hand slowly. "You're not in trouble, boy. I came here as a friend, not to arrest you," he said, sensing the fear continuing to rise in the young scanner. "You see, I happen to understand your 'problem.' And you may not know it, but there are others out there like you."

Others, David thought. What others? Who and where were these others Forrester was speaking of?

"A fair number, actually. You're not alone," Forrester added, smiling a grin that was full of false comfort.

The relief David felt at hearing Commander Forrester's words was matched only by the thankfulness he felt for the man. The weight of a lifetime of self-doubt and suspicion had, at last, been lifted. And this man was responsible. If he hadn't been a cop, he would have hugged him. Instead David only covered his face to hide his reaction.

The darkness of the small room at the institute made concentration easy. The testing lab allowed for no outside interference or noise.

As David stared into the camera before him, the sound of the shutter snapping was amplified hundreds of times, so still was the air in the room. When Dr. Morse eventually snapped on the lights, the glare temporarily blinded David, who blinked reactively as he was shown the Polaroid snapshots just taken.

"Your Kirlian photographs, David," Dr. Morse explained as he handed him the pictures. "This halo is an actual photograph of your psychic energy field. You give off extremely good vibes," he added with a laugh.

David was in no mood to even smile. After an entire morning of testing, his nerves were frayed and his curiosity piqued. Yet, even now, a pair of orderlies were placing more wires across his body.

"With this machine we're trying to measure your PSI, David," Dr. Morse continued. "That's short for Psychic Energy Waves. Just hold still. It won't take long," he explained.

Nodding his agreement, David held so still that he felt

every move of his breath inside his body. He felt tense, as if he might move in the wrong direction or at the wrong moment and invalidate the entire test.

As David attempted to relax, Dr. Morse activated the equipment. EKG patterns and oscilloscopes began to measure David's physiological parameters. Blood pressure, heartbeat, respiration, electrical conductivity, and brainwaves among them.

As the readings continued, Dr. Morse began to put David at ease, explaining how common his talents were to varying degrees in many people.

"Fifteen to twenty percent of the population have psychic powers of some kind, David," he said in a low, quiet voice. "Most of them undiscovered. They are what we call *receivers*. They're telepathically so sensitive that their brains function like cerebral radio antennae. They pick up other people's PSI waves, their thoughts, distant sounds."

"All those voices?" David questioned, remembering all too well the sounds that were growing louder and louder within his brain.

"A lot become schizophrenics," Dr. Morse explained. "The sheer volume of telepathic input causes severe pressure on the synapses, and consequent distortion. A small group we call *senders* can project their thoughts into the world," he said, lifting his arms in the air as if casting giant rose petals about. "And an even smaller number are both senders and receivers. Like you," he added, pointing in David's direction.

"Me. Why me?"

"Back in the fifties and sixties, an experimental drug called Ephemerol was prescribed to a sizable group of pregnant women. It was supposed to ease discomfort, but instead it caused an unusual birth defect. It created *scanners*."

"Can it be turned off?" David asked uneasily, looking around the room to make certain no one was listening.

"There's another drug, EPH-2," Dr. Morse offered. "It relieves the pressure and clears your mind. It even stops the headaches."

David could feel his burden lighten at the good news.

"But you don't want to take that drug," another voice intruded. It was Commander Forrester, who had heard their conversation as he quietly walked into the room. "Under no circumstances do you want to take that drug, David. It's very addictive. And the side effects can be devastating."

He again felt that Forrester was on his side, like he was warning him, looking out for his interests. Still, the pain in his head was unending.

"It's gotten so much stronger lately," he turned to Forrester to explain. "The last month has been like hell."

"It's probably just because you've never lived in the city before. In the country, everything was simpler, quieter, more gentle." David agreed, nodding his head as Forrester reminded him that the moral code in the country was stronger, the society more stable. "We sometimes lose our sense of values here."

"It's true, sir," David said looking first to Forrester then to Dr. Morse. "So my scanning ability didn't really *develop* here, it just became stronger."

"It was latent for the most part, but subconsciously, you used it," Morse said.

"That's what gave you your feeling toward animals," Forrester surmised.

"But, how did you guys know about that?" David asked slowly, suddenly suspicious again.

Forrester was ready. He picked up a thick police dossier and tapped his finger against the binder. His look suggested that he knew everything there was to know about David

Ketchum. Everything! While it was scary, it was reassuring at the same time. Surely, this man really will look out for my interests, David felt in his heart.

"Now what we want to do here is teach you to control your power," Forrester said as he walked over to David's chair, deliberately taking his mind off the question. "We want you to be able to use your power, and learn how to protect yourself from overload."

"Overload. I need to protect myself . . . from myself," David heard himself saying.

Forrester nodded his head in total understanding, while Dr. Morse smiled his warmest grin. Both men seemed to have the situation under control. They had won David's confidence; he was cooperative, and would prove so much more useful than Drak, whose problems were increasing every day.

The slamming open of the examination room door sent all eyes staring in that direction. There, silhouetted in the light from the hallway was Drak, looking like a new man. Dressed in a well-tailored suit and neatly combed hair, he looked like anything but a mental patient.

David was stunned when their eyes met. A chill went slowly up his spine and he felt the tiniest hairs standing up straight on his arms as he gazed at the demented scanner crossing the room toward him.

Sneering in David's direction, barely hiding an obvious dislike for the newcomer, Drak pushed a chair aside and leaned crudely against a counter.

"David, I'd like you to meet Steven Drak. He is also a scanner," Forrester said by way of introduction.

"So, the new lab rat," Drak laughed in David's direction. "They give you any of the magic potion yet, sweetie?"

"Steven has had a particularly difficult time dealing with his special talents," Forrester quickly interrupted. "We're trying to help him adapt to his new environment here."

"Yeah. They're lovely to me here," Drak grinned, picking at his teeth with his little finger. "Took me out to Louis's, bought me some new threads. Snappy, huh?" he said as he rolled his hand beneath the lapel.

David speechlessly watched the display before him. He wasn't sure exactly what Drak was, but he knew he didn't like him. And, more importantly, he never wanted to end up like him either.

Watching David's every movement, Drak pulled up a chair across the table from him, and with a twisted little sneer he zapped a tiny scan in his direction. The pain shot through David's skull like an electrical charge. For a split second it was there; and then nothing . . . except when he touched his nostril, he felt the dampness of blood.

"Steven!" shouted Dr. Morse. "You promised to co-operate."

"Maybe if I had one more shot," he laughed like a drunk on a binge. Pulling himself straighter in his chair and handing his handkerchief to David, he apologized, explaining, "I just need another shot, pal."

Morse was not amused. Seeing David's discomfort, he turned back to Drak. "You'll get one when we're finished here." Not wanting to alarm David further, the doctor walked over and placed his hand on the student's shoulder, apologizing once again for Drak's behavior.

"What pretty eyes you have, said the wolf," Drak hissed.

Scanning David in all-out war, Drak was unrelenting in his sting. David grabbed his temples in pain.

"Block his scan, David. Concentrate. You can do it," Dr. Morse encouraged.

Unsure exactly what to do, David began to fight the pain, attempting to push it, forcing it out of his head and back towards his enemy. Drak clearly had the upper hand, but David refused to submit. With blood running from his nose, his hands to his temples, he commanded all his concentration in Drak's direction. Gradually, Drak became aware that something was happening. He, too, felt the pressure that came with an intense scan; he, too, began to feel the blood vessels enlarge in his nostrils.

Forrester's smile matched that of Dr. Morse's. "Excellent," Morse said to David. "Now focus your scan. Link up with his nervous system. Gradually try to take control."

The two scanners were facing off like arm wrestlers of the mind. Ever so gradually, David turned up the pressure, adding intensity bit by bit. With each amplification of his scan, David felt the pressure in his own mind decreasing, a reward for a job well done.

Drak began to bleed from his ears and his nose, clenching his fists, grimacing grotesquely. He was trying to fight, but the scan was too strong, too deliberate, too even.

Drak screamed in pain, giving up the fight, grasping his head in tortured agony.

"I'm so sorry. I didn't mean to . . ." David said as he released his scan and rushed to Drak's side, trying his best to attempt to comfort him.

"Shit!" was the only word Drak uttered, without looking up. Suddenly, he jerked his head back, a look of twisted insanity in his eyes. Drak meant business. He would not give up.

Before he could retaliate, Dr. Morse stopped the little game. "Steven," he shouted. "Your shot . . ."

Obediently, Drak turned his attention toward the doctor, rising and following him out of the room like a trained puppy.

"You did very well, David," Forrester finally said.

"I didn't want to hurt him," David responded, obviously affected by what had just happened. Drifting into deep and troubled thought, David wished he were back on the farm, wrapped in the safety of his parents' arms.

"Well, this has been tiring," Forrester said, rubbing David's back in comfort. It felt good to the student to have someone care. Instinctively, David felt himself thinking that Forrester must be the most compassionate policeman in the entire city.

The local dairy plant had quite a reputation among its competitors. High efficiency, high yield, and high employee morale. It was an operation to be proud of. Until recently, that is. The recurrence of strychnine poisoning in milk products had caused demand to plummet and production to suffer.

Every employee was on edge, each a suspect in a heinous crime the likes of which the city had never seen, and the continuing efforts of the police force had made life around the plant more than uncomfortable. Until the criminal was captured and convicted, security would continue at intolerable levels. Every move was scrutinized, every assembly-line worker guilty until proven innocent.

The arrival of Police Commander Forrester wasn't helping matters. It was only moments after he drove up to the dairy plant that the entire facility was on alert. Forrester had come before, of course. But this time was different. This time he had brought an expert with him, a sort of human bloodhound.

As Commander Forrester and David Ketchum toured the plant, their guide was chief security officer Kelly, a loyal employee who was feeling the brunt of the recent pressure over the poisoning. Kelly couldn't help but feel that they were stepping on his turf. He could solve the mystery, if only he had more time. Time was now in short supply, however, with three young kids already dead because of the killer.

"This Milk Murderer is the lowest kind of criminal," Forrester had told David before they approached the plant. "Also the toughest for us to make. But in similar cases, the tamperer always turned out to be a disgruntled employee of the manufacturer's."

David pondered those words as they walked slowly past the executive offices and into the processing center.

"Just walk around. Make eye contact. *Concentrate*," Forrester whispered into David's ear, leaving him to his work.

Despite the fact that he was trying to look as inconspicuous as possible, David found every eye following his approach and departure. In a way that made it simpler. As each would look up in turn, David would hit them briefly with a scan, sensing their guilt or their innocence.

First one, then another. Each rubbing their noses after David's electrifying scan. He walked past the bottling room, the filling stations, the pasteurization vats—each as empty of suspects as the next.

It took several hours, and several false alarms, but finally David was certain. The killer was not here; not a worker in this plant.

He shook his head as he talked in hushed tones to Forrester as they left to deliver the news to Kelly and the company's president.

Along the way, David paused at the door to the dairy's front office. Inside a clerk sat silently behind a small desk, scowling as he worked.

His momentary glance in David's direction was all that

was needed. Neither David nor Forrester budged as he turned his back on the uninvited guests.

"Your name is Ralph Chaney," David said, completely surprising himself as well as the little clerk.

"Who are you, and what do you want?" came the reply from the startled little man.

"You've been working here for thirteen years," David said, continuing to read his mind. "You thought you should have been made manager, but you weren't. You don't think it's fair."

Chaney dropped any semblance of attitude and panicked. Pushing his accounting ledgers in David's direction, he attempted to charge toward the door. His feet felt like they have been glued to the floor, like nails held the soles of his shoes to the carpet.

"Get the hell out of here," Chaney screamed, attracting attention for all in the adjoining offices.

"That's why you injected those milk cartons with strychnine," David said, aware for the first time of the implications of his discovery. "Those poor children."

David's emotion welled to the surface now, and his concentration lapsed long enough for Chaney to break free of his scan. The elderly clerk charged out the door but he was no match for the college student in the foot-race down the hallway. When Chaney reached the exit door at the end of the hall, David was right behind him.

Reaching for the knob, Chaney felt the charge of a scan race through his body. Every nerve pulsated in excruciating pain.

"Stop, you murderer!" David ordered as the hallway filled with shocked workers.

Suddenly crumbling to his knees from the continuing strength of David's scan, Chaney was reduced to a mass of convulsing hysteria.

"All right. I did it!" he screamed. "Now, stop whatever it is you're doing. PLEASE," he begged.

"You did what, Mr. Chaney?" David asked, maintaining the intensity of his scan.

"I poisoned that milk . . . four dozen containers. I wanted to show the bastards. Make them pay for what they did to me."

As the security guards rushed to surround their co-worker, David looked across the room. On the opposite side nearest the door stood Forrester. The look of pride on his face convinced David that his powers could be used for justice; that perhaps he could play an important role in Forrester's new order of justice after all.

Later that night, his trip to the hospital seemed quicker than usual. Perhaps it was because he was reliving his triumph. Perhaps it was because now he knew more than ever that he was in love.

David parked his truck in his usual spot and made the familiar trek to the fourth floor where the nurses had grown accustomed to seeing the handsome young man bringing his bouquet of fresh flowers to Room 405.

As David entered the darkened room, Alice was sitting up reading a newspaper. Her smile matched David's as she held out her arms in greeting. Her kiss was warm and full of deep-felt affection.

She didn't dare tell him that he had been in nearly every thought she had all day, and how she had counted the hours until they would be together again. She wanted to be sophisticated; she wanted to be romanced. But her heart was so excited at the warmth of his embrace that she dropped any hope of pretense and blurted out exactly what she had been thinking since they were together last.

"Every time that door opened I hoped it was you," she whispered as their lips parted. "And every time, it was just another nurse with another pill or a thermometer or something equally as boring.'' He held her tight to his chest, her lips next to his ear. ''Don't leave me again. Ever. Let's just pretend for this very moment that all the ugliness and horror that happened was only a dream. Please say we can pretend it was all a dream, David.''

David's eyes began to mist as he thought how wonderful it would be if it were only that simple. To simply wish away those robbers and the killings and the blood. But the truth was far more real than any dream, made all the more spectacular by what had happened that very day.

''Alice, sweetheart, there's something I've got to tell you and it has nothing to do with dreams,'' he said, gazing into her eyes.

''David? What is it? There hasn't been more trouble has there?''

Rising from the bed, David reached into his pocket for the newspaper clipping it contained. ''I've been out working today, Alice,'' he said, slowly unfolding the piece of newsprint.

''Working? Doing what?'' she asked, a look of suspicion falling across her brow.

Rather than answer, David held up the newspaper. The front-page headline read: ''MILK MURDERER CONFESSES!'' She took the paper out of his hands, confused at his smile and the look of pride.

''I don't get it,'' she said, trying to put the pieces together and getting nowhere fast.

''I worked with the police. I'm the one who found him. The Milk Murderer. I made him confess,'' David said, sitting back on the bed, beaming now.

Alice wasn't smiling. She failed to see the connection. ''Are you serious? You?''

Almost euphoric with pride, yet wound tight just the

same, David stumbled across the words as he tried to make her understand. "Commander Forrester took me to the milk plant and I sort of . . . well, we walked around and I sort of . . . sorta read people's minds. It was strange. I used my powers and scanned the guy."

"Scanned," Alice repeated incredulously. If David was making sense, why was she having such a hard time understanding the point, she wondered silently.

"Scanned. You know. I used telepathy to read his mind, to see his thoughts. I scanned his brainwaves. I have this power. I was born with it. I'm a scanner."

Alice was stunned. If this was some sort of joke, she didn't find it funny. What she wanted was a normal boyfriend who might someday become a veterinarian. What she found before her was someone talking about reading minds and controlling thoughts. No, this couldn't be happening, she thought to herself. But with David around, she might as well have spoken the words.

"Don't think that," he said impulsively, sweeping her with a scan. "And don't be scared. It's good. It's wonderful. And, believe you me, I'm very relieved."

"Relieved?" Alice reacted, pushing herself away from him.

"Listen, Alice. All my life I've felt that there was something wrong with me. I had this secret problem. I felt ashamed, like a freak. There would be times when I was growing up that the other kids would tease me, unceasingly. They didn't know why, but they, too, knew I was different. And it was easier to laugh at what they didn't understand than to have compassion for what went unexplained . . ."

David lapsed into silence for a moment, his mind drifting back to a time years earlier, when the bitterness of childhood made life on the farm very lonely. "Now, Commander Forrester's made me see it isn't a problem at all.

It's a gift. And a very special one at that," David added, looking for some sort of approval from Alice.

"You mean . . . you actually mean you're going to use this power?" she asked, almost afraid to hear the answer.

"There's so much I can do," David urged. "Fighting crime is just the beginning. Don't you see?"

Actually, Alice did see the potential in David's amazing gift, but the thought of him getting involved with criminals scared her, keeping her from joining David's enthusiasm completely.

"It's amazing," was all she could say as she stared at this man-boy who had won her heart.

"No, you're amazing," he corrected, caressing her face gently, brushing the hair away from her cheek and slowly bending down to kiss it lightly.

Alice closed her eyes as he moved his mouth toward hers, feeling a little self-conscious despite the passion of the moment. This was, after all, a hospital, with doctors and nurses and orderlies around to make certain that she did nothing that would excite her or slow her healing in any way. Still, as she felt his warm breath nearing her lips, nothing seemed to matter except David.

Quite suddenly, she felt another feeling joining in tandem with her sexual arousal. It was a nervous tingle; an involuntary surge that made her uncomfortable. Uncomfortable enough to squirm slightly underneath David's touch.

"Just relax," she heard him saying. Opening her eyes, Alice felt David's presence inside her brain. Could he be scanning her, she wondered?

"David, what are you . . ." she began to say, before his fingers lightly sealed her lips in silence.

"Just relax. I want to try something," he said, and began to search her eyes in earnest.

His loving scan was incredible. Alice had never felt anything like it before. Despite the fact that she had dated often in college, and had had her share of boyfriends, this sensation was somehow larger than human experience. Thoughts raced through her mind; thoughts of her favorite things.

Her favorite pet—a dog named Wilson. Her father had given her the collie when she was only four. A rag doll that was her constant companion during the dark nights alone in her room. Her first kiss; she was only ten.

And now David. She saw him naked. Looking into her eyes smiling. A body so perfect that even the small mole beneath his right shoulder seemed to belong. While she had never minded imperfections in a man—in fact she often found them exciting—the pleasure David provided was from certain beauty. His body was showing no hint of future change. His skin was smooth and tight around sinewy muscle.

She found herself groaning quietly before snapping back to reality. "God, what are you doing to me?"

"Feel good?" David asked, smiling sensitively now.

"I'm almost embarrassed to say yes," Alice laughed, her voice low and catching unexpectedly in her throat. "I guess I was dreaming."

"You were only seeing thoughts of love," he replied, knowing full well that he had played a major role in her perceptions.

"What is going on in here," came the harsh voice of the nurse who had just pushed open the door. "Young man, you get yourself off of that bed, now!" she commanded, moving in David's direction. "Your time is up," she said.

How simple it was for David to fix her with a scan. A harmless glance in her direction and suddenly she was silent and unmoving. In another moment, she was turning, heading out the door, almost moving robotically, a certain stiffness in her walk, mechanically obeying his unspoken command.

As she closed the door behind her, both Alice and David couldn't help but laugh. Perhaps David's special gift would be more rewarding than he had ever imagined. The look on Alice's face suggested as much.

"Now, where were we," she teased in mock confusion.

"Let me see if I can remember," David smiled, lying down next to her in bed, the stubble of his beard just grazing her chin.

Visions of a field full of daisies popped into her mind. Dressed in white, she saw herself leaning against a tree as David rode into the foreground on a palomino stallion.

As her dream deepened, the only sound to be heard was the EKG monitor next to her bed, its audible beep sounding over and over with increasing speed, and passionate irregularity.

CHAPTER FIVE

FORRESTER

WAYNE FORRESTER—ANGRY AND ANXIOUS
By Daniel Eastburn

Wayne Forrester slams his fist into the desk pad and curses. It's the fourth time during our hour-long interview that his frustrations have rammed their way to the surface and exploded like lava bursting from a caldera. At these times, he is a man unleashed, wild in his intensity and totally unpredictable.

On the metropolitan police force for the past fifteen years, Forrester has risen through the ranks from beat cop to sergeant to lieutenant, and, finally, commander of the Fourth Precinct. Various medals and commendations line the walls of his office on the fifth floor of the Municipal Center, a fitting reminder of his contribution to the city he serves.

"They give you these plaques," Forrester says, having caught my eyes staring over his shoulder to the wall beyond, "as if to justify the fact that they can't or won't deal with the real situation. Crime is out of control in this city and the money isn't there to fight it effectively. Damn the bureaucrats with misplaced priorities," Forrester adds as if to emphasize his point. His vibrato matches his mood as his voice raises in pitch and volume.

Defense of his department and his men comes quickly. This is his family, he leaves little doubt. Having graduated from the police academy as his father did before him, Forrester was engaged to Annette Warner, a childhood sweetheart. Her sudden death in a hit-and-run accident only days before the wedding left a wound which healed slowly, helped along by devotion to his work. Since that time, Forrester has been credited with spearheading campaigns to increase the size of the police force and its responsibilities; he's met only moderate success but is unending in his resolve.

His surprise election as president of the Police Benevolence League suggests a man driven to push the power and scope of law enforcement to its extremes. As such, Forrester is a man with many critics, his outspoken nature contributing to his controversial image within the police community.

"There are those who would like to see me shut up and hide," Forrester suggests in characteristic honesty. *"Yet, they are the same people who will come running to me at the first suggestion that criminals are starting to get the upper hand."*

Wayne Forrester—an angry and anxious servant of the people.

Police Commissioner Mitchell Stokes stood leaning over the sink in his bathroom, his potbelly hanging over the edge of the tiled counter, his pajama top absorbing the water splashing from the faucet. With one end of a piece of dental floss in each hand, he positioned himself closer to the light, pulling the thread between his back molars.

He hadn't always taken care of his teeth. But lately he had been on a health regime, partly due to his increase in weight, partly due to a new secretary in City Hall. Glancing at one side and then the other, Stokes decided that his body was in pretty good shape for someone in his late fifties. Yessir. A few pounds off around the middle and that new secretary would be putty in his hands.

As the police commissioner flushed the used floss down the toilet, he thought he heard a noise over the swirling water. He listened closer, and decided it was nothing. Nothing at all, he reasoned. Walking slowly back to the sink, he began to wonder if hearing sounds was the first sign of senility setting in.

The toothbrush was barely loaded with his favorite Colgate when Stokes heard the noise again. This time he was certain it wasn't senility. It sounded like a dull dragging sound coming from the attic of his house.

Taking the precaution of loading his .44, he held the handgun close to his side and ventured quietly out of the bedroom, down the long, dimly lighted hallway. The walls were covered with commendations from various local clubs, and their shadows cast eerie designs across the striped wallpaper.

Gripping his gun tighter now, he turned toward the attic door, stopping to listen as the noise continued. It reminded him of the sound that a car makes when it drags a cardboard box underneath its chassis. A raspy sort of sound that he couldn't quite make out.

Opening the door in the hallway, Stokes began to climb up the old, unpainted wooden steps. Each creaked under the weight of his body, announcing his arrival on the scene. The attic door at the top of the stairway was slightly ajar. Unusual, he thought. He always kept it shut to prevent drafts in the clapboard house.

Pushing open the door with the barrel of his gun, Stokes entered the dark attic, pausing only briefly to turn on the light. The low-watt bulb hanging by a wire from the ceiling did little in the way of real illuminating. It provided only slightly more light than a candle, but Stokes knew this attic's every corner, so he wasn't concerned.

The place had a rather childlike quality to it, helped along by all the toys peering curiously from the tops of opened boxes. Dust was everywhere, it seemed, casting its own pall of gloom upon all it touched. As he moved down past a crate of old books, Stokes brushed against an old rocking horse, scaring himself in the process.

Thinking how silly he must look—a police commissioner in his wet pajamas in the attic being scared by a wooden horse—he laughed despite the tension filling his body. Searching the darkness, Stokes sensed a presence. Extending his gun, he panned from one side of the room to the other, looking for movement in the shadowy silhouettes.

At last he heard it. A raspy breathing coming from the

far side of the room. "Whoever you are, step out or I'll shoot!" he shouted, moving not a muscle.

"No need for that, Commissioner," came a reply from the darkness.

Stokes's heart pumped wildly as he saw a figure step into the hazy light casting its glow before him.

"The name is Drak, Commissioner," the unearthly man announced brazenly, walking closer now to stare the policeman squarely in the face.

"I don't care what your name is. You're under arrest," Stokes said, still pointing the .44 toward Drak's head. "Get down on the floor. Keep your hands where I can see them!"

Drak didn't move, preferring to give Stokes a smartass grin deliberately aimed at intimidation. "I've got a better idea. I stay here, you stay there," Drak mocked.

Instantly, Stokes felt his body hit by some sort of electrifying force, causing him to freeze in his tracks, unable to even pull the trigger. Pressure began to build in his head. He could actually feel the blood vessels pounding in his brain.

Trying to fight the paralyzing effect, Stokes shuffled slightly to his left, shaking his head.

"Now open your mouth," Drak teased in babytalk like a parent telling a child to take medicine.

Stokes's jaw dropped open and his eyes widened in amazement at his lack of control over the situation.

"Now, put the gun under your tongue," Drak instructed in singsong fashion, obviously enjoying his power over the old, balding man before him. With hideous amusement, he laughed as Stokes was helpless but to obey.

As if in a trance, yet fully aware of what he was doing, Stokes slowly placed the barrel of the gun inside his mouth. The cold steel edged itself into the sensitive wet flesh of his cheek. Helpless, yet obeying, Stokes involuntarily began to shake, his entire body a mass of exposed nerve endings.

"Good, Mitchy. Now pull the trigger-wigger," mocked Drak.

Stokes's finger tensed on the trigger as he fought with all the strength left in him to battle against the scan. Drak, sensing that Stokes was stronger than he originally had thought, merely smiled as he increased the intensity of his telepathy.

"I said pull it!" Drak yelled, suddenly angry.

Clearly overpowered, Stokes yelled a final scream of opposition as he quickly pulled the trigger. Pieces of flesh exploded across the room as his body was sent smashing into some glass panes neatly leaning against the wall in the corner. Blood drained from his body; then, he violently jerked for several seconds before death offered its own form of mercy.

The look on Drak's face expressed nothing but pleasure.

There was another kind of look on the face of Police Commander Wayne Forrester when he burst into Alice's hospital room the next morning. It was one of anticipation.

Wearing his best dress-uniform complete with a chestful of medals, a pair of mirrored sunglasses, and a new slicked-back hairdo, Forrester swaggered into the room anxious to be noticed.

The fact that both David and Alice were lying naked on the bed still fast asleep mattered little. In fact, he rather appreciated the picture, pausing for a long moment to absorb the sight of their flesh pressed one against the other before walking over and noisily snapping open the drapes that darkened the room.

Startled by the light and the sound, David shot awake. He sat up quickly and covered Alice protectively. "What the hell," he shouted at no one in particular. Sensing someone else in the room, Alice gave out a muffled shriek and pulled the covers over her head.

"Now settle down, Davey," Forrester said, walking over toward the bed and tossing David his pants.

"Commander Forrester?" David said, still groggy with sleep. "Alice, Commander Forrester is here."

"Well, tell him to go away," she said from her sheet-shrouded hiding place.

"Now, now, you kids. I'm sorry to disturb you, but this is an emergency. David, you have to come with me, right now. I'll explain on the way," Forrester said.

David was suspicious but still rose out of bed. He had never seen the police commander so dressed up or excited. It wasn't until he was in Forrester's car that he heard about the death of Police Commissioner Stokes.

"It was so unexpected, David. None of us thought of the commissioner as suicidal," Forrester was saying as he steered his car toward City Hall. "I was just speaking to him last week, as a matter of fact, and he seemed to be in such good spirits. I'm devastated, as you can imagine," he added, turning to look at David.

The scanner was still trying to completely absorb the tragedy of events that had occurred the night before. The police commissioner apparently was so secretly despondent that he had taken his service revolver and blown his brains out. The thought sent shivers down David's spine. Even though he had never personally met the man, he had great compassion for anyone in that kind of mental torment.

The two parked at City Hall, aware that the number of news vans out front suggested the mob scene they would find inside. Forrester was not disappointed. As he approached the auditorium, he was surrounded by curious reporters asking him to speculate on the police commissioner's death. David was all but pushed into the background as he tried to keep up.

"It is a terrible tragedy," Forrester kept repeating as he walked through the crowd. "I have no further comment." At last he felt like he was getting the recognition he deserved. Finally, these reporters would learn who really could take control of this city.

As he entered the auditorium, he paused at the door to give David a press pass and show him to a seat in the front row. Directly to their left, news anchor Carole White was reporting live on the air, her voice echoing in the hall around them.

"We are all awaiting the arrival of Mayor Franzoni," White spoke into her hand microphone as she faced the camera. "The mayor will confirm the apparent suicide of Police Commissioner Mitchell Stokes, we're told, as well as announce the appointment of his immediate successor."

Forrester seemed to be preoccupied, David thought, as he noticed the Commander's fingers tapping nervously on his chair.

"Sources close to the mayor have confirmed to this reporter that her choice will be Vice Commissioner Norman Yancy," White said. The sound of those words seemed to stun Forrester; his eyes glazed over and his expression was tight with determination.

"Yancy is soft, David," Forrester turned and said to him quietly, cupping his mouth with his hand to ensure privacy. "He's not a leader; he's not a doctor. He can't cure anything. Under him, the city will just get sick and perhaps die. Cities die, sometimes, did you know that,

David? New York is dead, Los Angeles . . ." He paused, smiling suddenly, as if remembering something from his past.

David was perplexed by Forrester's strange behavior. In the short time he had known Commander Forrester, he had always seemed so levelheaded, so directed. But Forrester's bringing him here—no, more than that, insisting that he come—was just plain weird, he thought to himself.

"You don't always see cities dying right away, you know that, don't you David. But when the rot closes around the very heart, then it's too late."

Feeling very uncomfortable in the front row of this official press conference wearing a press badge, David began to instinctively look around the room, trying to take his mind off of what Forrester was saying. Yet, try as he might, his mind insisted that he return to study the police commander's face.

"David, don't let our city die," Forrester continued. "I want you to scan the mayor."

Now, obviously alarmed, David did his best to protest. "This isn't right. She was elected. I can't . . ."

"If we don't do it, no one will," Forrester interrupted, grabbing David's forearm and squeezing tightly into his flesh. "We did all right at the dairy the other day, didn't we?"

David reluctantly nodded, still unconvinced. "But . . ."

"Trust me," Forrester added quickly, releasing his grip and turning his attention to the podium onstage as the mayor made her entrance without fanfare.

"Good morning to you all and thank you for coming. I am certain by now you have all heard the tragic news of last evening. I deeply mourn the death of my dear friend,

Commissioner Mitchell Stokes,'' Mayor Franzoni began, speaking in a somber tone. "We are shocked and grieved by his sudden departure.''

Forrester leaned in closer to get nearer to the mayor, as if listening intently; he silently signalled David to do the same.

"Because of the crucial nature of the vacant post and the present circumstances of the city, I, as mayor, believe it is necessary to appoint an acting police commissioner without delay.''

Forcefully grabbing David's arm again, Forrester whispered loudly into his ear. "Now. Do it now.''

David hesitated, unsure of what to do. Using his power to intercept the brainwaves of a criminal was one thing; interfering in the duties of a publicly elected official was something else entirely.

Though he was focusing on the mayor, David felt Forrester's grip now painfully tight around his arm. Like a tourniquet, the hold was stopping the flow of blood to his hand.

"Therefore . . .'' The mayor continued, then she paused to look down as if she had suddenly lost her place in her notes. "Therefore,'' she repeated. Looking up, she found her eyes meeting David's; she was caught in his gaze, drawn to his eyes like a hummingbird to the nectar of sweet flowers. Almost instinctively.

David centered his scan and locked it in place, the silent maneuver known only to him. As he took control, he noticed the mayor wince momentarily, obviously in discomfort.

"Therefore, I am naming an interim successor . . .'' she continued, slowly, deliberately.

The city hall press attache glanced across at Vice Commissioner Norman Yancy, who was nervously shuffling his prepared acceptance speech, a slight layer of moisture beginning to collect on his forehead.

He glanced into the audience where his wife of twenty-two years was sitting proudly, though obviously still in shock at the loss of their dear friend. Yancy had known Mitch Stokes since they both attended the police academy together. At one point, they were even partnered on a foot patrol.

Stokes had been godfather to Yancy's two children, and he mourned the loss of his trusted colleague like few others could. Adding to his feeling of helplessness was the unexpected nature of Stokes's violent death. He refused to accept the suggestion that his friend had committed suicide; it was simply not a possibility in Yancy's book.

He had already placed several detectives on the case, convinced that somehow foul play was involved. Even as he sat anxiously awaiting the announcement of his appointment as acting police commissioner, he wondered why such a senseless death had marred their lives.

The mayor hesitated again, pausing to touch her head and ease the migraine she was experiencing. "Excuse me," she said apologetically before continuing. "Let me introduce our acting police commissioner . . ."

"Do it," Forrester insisted, turning to face David and trying to use his own version of mental telepathy to push the student into action.

"Commander Wayne Forrester," the mayor announced hesitantly.

Behind the mayor, both Vice Commissioner Yancy and the press attache were stunned. Even as they eyed each other in total disbelief, Forrester was jumping from his seat to join them on stage.

Even the most jaded among the reporters in attendance seemed to be shocked by the mayor's sudden change of heart. As she stepped back away from the microphone, she looked weak and seemed unable to catch her breath. Sitting down, the mayor dabbed at her nose gently with her handkerchief, noticing a small spot of blood. The room was full of scattered whispers by the time Forrester reached the podium.

"Thank you, Ms. Mayor. I am truly honored," he began, beaming as the mayor was helped off the stage by her assistant. "The other night on television, I said this city needed a new order. Now the mayor, in her wisdom, has given me a chance to provide it. And I thank her."

David sat silently watching his friend make his acceptance speech, feeling suddenly guilty about all that had taken place. He began to feel sick to his stomach and tried to quietly leave the room.

Even as David rose, Forrester directed his comments in his direction. "I'm going to begin by giving the streets of the city back to the people, the decent people, the human beings," he said. As David sat back down in his seat, he wondered if Forrester was excluding him in his description.

"Our environment is polluted. Not just the air and water and the food that we eat, but our social environment as well. Man has become an endangered species. I want to preserve him. I give the people of this city my word. I will start a new order, a new war against crime."

This was more than David could stand. Holding his stomach he quickly exited the auditorium, rushing past the reporters and the cameramen, whose lenses were trained on Forrester.

In the hallway, he could hear Forrester speaking about pride in the city and how each and every citizen would be called upon to do his part in combating the plague of crime that was rampant. He tried to block the rhetoric that seemed to be droning on and on.

As he reached the doorway to the street, he realized he was not alone. Turning instinctively, his eyes met those of Drak's—cold, foreboding in their darkness.

"So you passed the big test, huh, Davey," Drak goaded. "The bigshot did his thing and no one is the wiser."

"Out of my way," David retorted, not wanting to hear sarcasm or anything else from this creep. Drak looked even weirder than usual. He had lost a tremendous amount of weight, and his skin had taken on a grayish hue. The effects of the EPH-2 addiction were taking their toll.

"He said he would get you to do it," Drak continued, still blocking the doorway, sneering and hissing the words out of his mouth.

David pushed past him, unable to listen to what was obviously the truth.

Following quickly behind him, Drak yelled in his direction, "You ever scan Forrester? Better than a splatter film. You know how his 'new order' works? They use scanners to control the society. Starting here and going . . . to the moon, Alice. To the moon."

David refused to believe what he was hearing. Forrester was good. Forrester wanted criminals off the street so that violence would be a thing of the past. He didn't want to control. That couldn't be his plan, David thought to himself.

"You're crazy, Drak," David turned and screamed, aware that he was losing all control.

"Maybe so," Drak countered, finally catching up to David, gasping for lack of breath. "Maybe I'm crazy, but I'm not wrong."

David stared at him in disbelief. Drak couldn't be right. He just couldn't.

"Don't believe me? Check out the scanners in Morse's basement," Drak told him. "Because if you don't work out for Forrester, baby, that's your new address."

David pulled himself away, turning and running down the sidewalk, past news vans, past the parade of customers entering and exiting the post office. Reaching the corner, David felt tears streaming down his face. What had he done? David's mind was reeling in confusion. If Drak could possibly be right, he had set a monster loose within the city. He had to discover the truth, and discover it now.

David thought about what Drak had said all that day. He walked for hours, never going anywhere and never reaching anyplace in particular. By the time he arrived at the hospital later that night to pick up Alice, he was torn by indecision. It would be wonderful having her home again, that much he knew for certain. Yet seeing the innocence in her eyes, he was ashamed of what he had done, unsure of whether he should confide in her.

The short drive home seemed endless. Silence muted every thought and kept speech to a minimum. Alice knew something was very wrong, but David seemed distant, unable to concentrate. She tried being charming . . . inquisitive . . . defensive. Yet, nothing worked to pierce the outer protective shell David had pulled around his thoughts.

Pulling into her driveway and seeing her home again brought Alice close to tears. Being forced to be away makes one appreciate the pleasures of being back home, she thought as David unloaded her suitcase from the truck-bed.

Trooper greeted them both with barks and licks after running around in circles in the kitchen to show his excitement at Alice's return. Not even Trooper was able to gain a response from David. The strain was reaching the breaking point, and both of them knew it.

After making Alice comfortable in her own bed, David tenderly placed Trooper next to her and caressed the dog gently. Suddenly, his eyes filled with tears. Alice was stunned and confused by David's grief.

Without direction, sometimes rambling, David slowly unraveled the secrets of the day to the one person he knew he could trust.

Alice's increased expression of alarm didn't help his confidence when he told her that he was responsible for Forrester's appointment. And not even feeling her warm body next to his made his mind feel at ease.

There was only one thing to do. Return to the institute and learn the truth. Instantly Alice protested. There was no way that she would allow him to return to that place unprotected. David knew the danger, of course, but not even Alice's attempts at persuasion were going to change his mind. As he patted Trooper's head and kissed Alice goodbye, he wondered in his heart if he would ever see them again.

Forrester and Dr. Morse sat watching the eleven o'-clock news on the television in the institute's lounge. The antenna had recently been knocked down during a storm, so there were multiple images on the screen and the color was dimmer than either would have liked. Yet the message was coming across loud and clear. The mayor was as confused over her announcement earlier in the day as her staff was.

"Following her press conference," the newscaster was reporting, "Mayor Franzoni was unavailable to comment concerning the unexpected appointment, but her office did confirm that Wayne Forrester would likely be replaced in the near future by her permanent selection for commissioner of police.

"That's what she thinks," Forrester said as he rose

from his chair to turn off the set. "Now do you see what a clean scanner can do for us?" he asked Morse directly.

"He worked out this time," the doctor replied, remaining unconvinced. "But I'm not sure how long we can control him."

"Just you leave David to me," Forrester shot back. "We have a, shall we say, 'special' relationship."

"I wouldn't be too sure of that," Morse frowned, pointing to the security monitor near the ceiling of the office. David's truck had just pulled up to the guard gate outside, and Dr. Morse recognized an enemy in action.

The burly guard at the gate started up to the truck and then seemed to be immobilized in place as David drove past without the slightest difficulty.

"Obviously your 'special' friend is getting a little too clever with his talent, Forrester," Morse said tersely, following the truck on the monitor as it made its way to the main administration building.

Once inside, David had no trouble immobilizing the guard at the reception desk. One quick scan and the man was as motionless as if cast in granite. Dr. Morse knew that he had only seconds to summon more help. He moved across the room to hit the silent alarm button.

Before he even reached the alarm, a sharp rap on the door diverted his attention. Without waiting for an invitation, David entered the room, met by forced smiles on the faces of both Forrester and Morse.

"Is something the matter, David?" Dr. Morse asked, inching closer to the alarm button.

"That's what I'm here to find out," David answered, aware of the sharp tone of his voice.

Forrester picked up the mood and attempted to disarm it. "You're upset about what happened today. I admit, it was unorthodox."

Not about to be conned once again, David boldly moved directly in front of Forrester, head to head. "You're damn right I'm upset. And I want to know what's really going on here."

Forrester was alarmed as he felt the first tingle of a scan in his head. "David, stop it for God's sake," he shouted, turning his eyes away. "I have nothing to hide!"

Continuing his scan, David was stunned at what he discovered—stunned at the sickness he saw in Forrester's mind.

Forrester was gasping for breath, his nose starting to bleed, as the office door burst open and Feck pivoted in with a tranquilizer gun.

"Turn it off, you asshole!" he screamed in David's direction.

He tried to fire but was blocked by David's scan. Paralyzed in place, he could neither move nor defend himself.

Dr. Morse seized the opportunity to reach hastily for the tranquilizer pistol in his desk drawer. Pulling the trigger, a dart hit David in the bicep before he could scan and protect himself.

Grasping at the dart and yanking it out of the soft muscle tissue before the drug could begin to take effect, David scanned Morse to the floor near Forrester, the two men crying for help.

Spinning about quickly now, David knew he was obviously being outgunned and overpowered. As he moved to deliver another scan in Forrester's direction, Feck made a surprise assault from the rear, placing a full nelson around David's neck, pinning his body.

Still in pain, Forrester slowly pulled himself off the floor, picking up Morse's fallen pistol nearby. His eyes were filled with rage as he carefully cocked the pistol and placed the cold steel barrel against David's neck.

"Never, ever, question my authority. Do you hear me!" he screamed at David, who struggled against the threat. "And never, ever, scan me! Ever."

David was outraged at Forrester's egomaniacal display of temper. So Drak was right after all. The entire foundation of the new order was nothing more than a dictatorship in which Forrester was in charge of everything and everyone.

He had been duped; there could be no question now. How he hated this man hissing in his face, giving him orders as if he were his property to control and direct. Weary of the fight and beginning to feel the effect of the tranquilizer in his system, David nevertheless refused to compromise his position of strength.

Glaring back into Forrester's eyes, he merely shook his head. "It won't work. This new order of yours. It won't work, Forrester," he slurred.

"And why not?" Forrester retaliated.

A hidden reserve of defiance surged forth as David raised his head. "Because I won't let it," he announced, defying any and all in the room.

Refusing to concede defeat, David scanned Forrester back across the room with a bolt that sizzled through the man's trunk like lightning. As he slammed into the bookcase lining the wall, the pistol was knocked from his grasp and slid across the floor.

Strength surging through his body, David planted his right elbow firmly in Feck's ribs. He twisted as he landed his blow and escaped the junkie's grasp in one swift move.

"Stop him!" Morse yelled, seeing David lunging for the pistol on the floor before him.

Diving across the slick linoleum and nearly sliding into Forrester in the process, David grabbed for the tranquilizer gun. In a single motion he turned and fired into the hulking scanner heading toward him. Spinning again, David took aim and shot another dart at Forrester before turning and running out of the office for his life.

David ran down the hallway past door after door of examining rooms fearing any moment the full effect of the tranquilizer dart would hit him, engulfing him in a dreamlike netherworld from which there would be no awakening. Deciding the elevator would be too confining and too slow, David plowed through the stairway door, leaping two steps at a time. First one floor, then the next, climbing toward the lobby level, his breath nearing exhaustion. Finally, David reached his goal.

Crossing the reception area, he heard the alarm sound in shocking shrillness. With time running out, he darted toward the front door just as two guards made their way from the elevator. Dropping them in their place with a forceful scan, David felt his legs beginning to buckle underneath him.

"Damn that tranquilizer," he said under his breath as he lunged through the door and headed toward his truck. His heart beating in syncopated rhythm and every fiber of his body on alert, David made a final dash to the protection of his four-wheeler. Twice he slipped on the gravel driveway, twice he picked himself up and commanded his body to keep moving.

When he finally reached the cab of his truck, he was barely was able to pull himself inside, so drained of energy was every muscle in his body. He turned on the ignition, the sounds of the pursuing guards spurring him onward. He had to make it through the gate and to the main highway to safety.

The guard gate ahead was suddenly awash in activity. Gruner had appeared from nowhere, mobilizing the remaining guards on duty. Several were using their very bodies to block David's path. As Gruner himself moved to the front of the pack, David floored his accelerator, aiming straight for the crowd.

Without even aiming, Gruner fired at the oncoming truck in a desperate attempt to slow its speed. The bullets shattered David's windshield, its glass now a cobweb of broken pieces barely holding together against the force of the blowing night air.

Bursting through the closed gate, David eyed his rearview mirror. Gruner and his comrades were furiously screaming at one another for allowing his escape. Gaining speed, he steered his truck down the remote road toward the main highway. With each passing mile, his eyes became heavier and his muscles softer as he fought against the effect of the tranquilizer dart.

Inside the institute, Forrester, too, was reeling from the drug's effect. He was sweating profusely, and it was all he could do to dial Gelson's private number and hold on long enough for his operative to answer. "Gelson," Forrester said in a thick, slow voice. "David Ketchum is loose. I want him back. And I want him back alive!"

As the final word left his lips, he was already passing out on the office floor.

C H A P T E R   S I X

THE FARM

"This is a city in shock," said news reporter Carole White, facing the television camera, on location outside of City Hall. "First, the devastating death of Police Commissioner Mitchell Stokes two nights ago. Then, the unexpected appointment of Police Commander Wayne Forrester as acting police commissioner by Mayor Franzoni, followed by mixed signals coming from the mayor's office concerning the motivation behind her decision. With me now is Vice Commissioner Norman Yancy, who has agreed to update us on the current situation."

"Thank you, Carole. I join you in recalling my surprise

at the mayor's decision to appoint Police Commander Wayne Forrester as this city's acting police commissioner," Yancy said, directing his response to the news reporter. *"It is an appointment over which the mayor has already admitted dissatisfaction, and, at best, it will be a temporary measure. But please remember that Commander Forrester has been a devoted servant of the people of this city for over a decade, and, despite having voiced some rather dramatic concepts on how to decrease crime on our streets, he is a competent police officer.*

"Our goals in this matter are identical. All of us want an end to the current crime wave which has taken its toll on our nerves and resources. To that end, I welcome Commander Forrester and wish him well. The mayor has made it clear to me, however, that any move toward establishing a so-called new order within her administration will be discouraged at all costs. I join Mayor Franzoni in calling for patience and understanding on the part of your viewers. We will lick this situation just as we have overcome other difficulties in our growth."

"Thank you, Vice Commissioner," White said, turning her attention back to the camera. *"Yet, despite reassurances from City Hall, government officials and citizens alike remain concerned after the events which have taken place during the past forty-eight hours. Councilwoman Marilyn Richards has ordered a fullscale investigation into the actions of the mayor's office and requested funds for independent counsel to be assigned to the case. From City Hall, this is Carole White."*

The cool night air blasting against his face was the only thing keeping David Ketchum awake. Pulling off the highway at a roadside cafe, he stumbled from the cab of his truck just long enough to remove the tire iron from behind the driver's seat and smash the remainder of his windshield out of his way, clearing his vision and giving the air better access.

It was remarkable that he had managed to stay awake this long. He had been driving for at least an hour now, and fighting the effects of the tranquilizer had taken every bit of energy his body was able to deliver. He found singing helped the most. Songs from his past suddenly were flying from his mouth as he returned to the highway. He was intent on making it as far away from the institute as he possibly could.

His only lingering thoughts were for Alice. As he sat, his body propped against the steering wheel, his eyes barely able to track the road, he recalled how they first met. He remembered those first moments of each class when he was rapt with anticipation, waiting for her to walk into the room.

He realized now that there could be no going back. No more college, no more dormitory, but most important, no more Alice. He couldn't put her life in jeopardy; he owed her more than that.

Her memory tugged at his conscience; their moments together were so brief yet so special. He had to let her know how he felt while he was still able.

"Alice, Alice," he kept muttering to himself, his head weaving from side to side right along with the truck. His mind was beginning to numb and he knew it. He couldn't go on much longer. He had to find a telephone and quickly.

Spinning the truck around and heading back in the opposite direction, he set his sights back on that roadside coffee shop. He commanded his body to stay awake, forcing his mind to concentrate on the road, his only task to reach that phone he saw outside that dive—what was it called? Valma's Place. No, Valerie's Place. That was it.

Horns beeped his mind back to reality as he drifted

into a semiconscious state. He was running off the road with regularity now, depending on the sound of the tires on the gravel soft-shoulder to stir him awake.

He finally reaching the cafe and pulled off the road, carefully avoiding the particles of windshield left from his last visit. He stumbled to the pay phone and sloppily, almost unable to stand, he punched the 0 button and waited for an operator.

"Operator two-nine-six. How may I help you?" David heard.

"I'd like . . . to . . . make a . . . . make a collect call," David answered slurring his words slowly. He deliberately, and exactly, gave the operator Alice's number, knowing she would accept the charges.

"David! Oh, David. What's happened? Where are you? I've been watching the news and they've reported a break-in at the institute," Alice said in a rush.

"Alice . . . . Lisss . . . en to-o me," David said weakly into the phone. "I'm okay, baby, but . . ." and then he fell silent.

"David! Speak to me!"

Breathing deeply, David felt new life fill his lungs. "Tranquilizer. They hit me with a tranquilizer dart. I'm going home . . . home. I won't let them hurt you. Alice . . ." The receiver went dead.

Alice stared at the disconnected line in disbelief. She was panicked by the thought of her friend enduring the physical and mental torment which men of science and justice had wreaked upon him. She wanted him home; she wanted him here; she wanted him now in the worst way.

At first she thought about calling the police. She would explain what had happened to David and have them put out an APB for his own protection. Then, she thought of having to describe scanners and EPH-2, and knew she wouldn't be believed. Especially now that Forrester was in charge of the entire police department.

For the first time in her life, Alice felt completely helpless. She had nowhere to turn; no way to help. Her last thought as she drifted restlessly off to sleep was of the danger ahead for her special friend.

A loud banging on her door jolted Alice out of a bad dream. Glancing at her clock in a post-sleep fog she had difficulty focusing on its hands. Could it actually read 3:35 A.M., she wondered as she drew it nearer.

Whoever was knocking had no intention of leaving, of that she was certain. And Trooper had no intention of letting the person in. He danced and jumped and scratched at the door as he barked protectively.

Pulling on her robe, Alice made her way through the darkened room, turning on her kitchen light before drawing her curtain slightly to look out the window. Hoping against hope that David might have made it back to her, Alice was shocked to see the face of a policeman smiling back on the other side of the glass.

He was holding his badge high as further proof that he was a cop and that his visit was official. Opening the door a crack, Alice was appalled to see a thin, pale, and rather ugly stranger at his side.

"Sorry to wake you, Miss Leonardo," the officer said, his hand pushing on the door as if to gain entry. "I'm Lieutenant Gelson, and this is my colleague, Mr. Drak."

Alice didn't like their visit at this hour any more than she liked their looks. Staring into Drak's eyes was like seeing a horror movie come to life. As much as she tried, she couldn't seem to escape his gaze.

"We're looking for David Ketchum, miss. We thought you might know his present whereabouts."

Smiling, Alice thought the two men must be crazy or possessed or worse. Even if she knew exactly where David was, these guys would be the last, the very last, people she would tell the information to. "N-no . . . I have . . . no idea," she stuttered in response.

"Oh, really," Drak said, pushing past Gelson and Alice into the kitchen.

"Now just a minute, Mr. . . . ah, Drak. Was that your name?" Alice challenged. "No one invited you into my house. Now I suggest you leave, before I—"

"—before you what? Call the police," Drak laughed in her face.

Alice felt a sudden sharp pain in her temples. No novice to being scanned, she recognized the signs. Turning away from Drak and facing Lieutenant Gelson, she repeated, "Get out of my house, both of you. Now!"

But she was already too late. As quickly as the pain of the scan came, it was gone. Drak had done his handiwork and their mission was a success.

"It's okay. We're finished here," he sneered as he pushed his way outside once again.

"Sorry to bother you, miss," Gelson said as he exited, closing the door behind him.

Alice shuddered as she felt their presence again, despite the fact that they were no longer there. Evil has a way of lingering, she thought. As she flattened herself against the door, her eyes closed to the torment around her, she heard Drak speaking to Lieutenant Gelson. His words would echo in her heart forever:

"He went home. To Vermont."

What had she done.

The sun was just beginning to rise over the green hills of Vermont as David's truck made its way across the state line and into the prettiest farm country this side of Oklahoma. Tiny clapboard churches and small New England towns gradually gave way to rolling stretches of green farmland filled mostly with cattle and potatoes.

David's truck looked as if it had been in a battle. The windshield was now totally absent; pieces of glass and spots of dried blood still clung to the window frame, scratches and dents had almost destroyed the front grill and fenders.

Behind the wheel and still awake, David was actually feeling somewhat better now. Having fought the effect of the tranquilizer dart and won, he was gaining a renewed strength from the victory. The countryside was helping. The fresh crisp air, coming off the morning dew, acted like an energizer to his system.

The familiar sights he passed by brought back bittersweet memories as he traveled the final few miles to his parents' farm: the Miller place where he fell out of the apple tree and broke his front tooth; the old Presbyterian church, now boarded up and abandoned, where he played hide-and-seek in the bell tower; the green-leaf maple in Old Man Fenster's yard, which still proudly displayed the carved initials of his first love.

Turning up the long dirt road to the Ketchum farm, his truck aimed itself directly into the sun, which was putting on a fancy welcoming show in varying shades of orange and gold as it graced the tops of the lush trees.

As David pulled his truck up beside the old white-framed farmhouse that was home, he hardly had time to kill the engine before his parents were out the back door running to greet him.

A spry couple in their mid-sixties, George and Susan Ketchum were not prepared for what they saw. Their once handsome son was now weathered and pale. The long trip and continuous exposure to the air had burned his skin into a parched leathery texture.

David stepped slowly from his truck, extending his arms in welcome, then he collapsed on the ground from exhaustion. It would be hours before he would wake, comfortably pillowed in his old bed.

"You gave us a good scare, boy," his father said, sitting next to David's bed. "Your ma here nearly had me drive clear into town to fetch the doc. But I told her that we Ketchum's got tough skin, all right."

"Don't listen to your father," Susan Ketchum teased as she entered the room with some cups of steaming hot chocolate.

"Mom, Dad. We have to talk. And I know you'll answer me honestly," David said, taking a cup of hot chocolate and sipping it gradually. "When you were pregnant with me, Mother, you took a drug called Ephemerol, didn't you?"

Susan Ketchum shook her head, puzzled by the question. "What are you talking about? What drug? Ephem . . . what did you say?"

"Ephemerol, Mother. It made me what I am. It caused the birth defect."

"Birth defect? What birth defect you talking about, son?" David's father asked, wrinkling his brow as he searched for an answer.

"Quit treating me like a child," David exploded, ready to hear the truth and not seeing it in his parents' eyes. "Just tell me the truth, dammit!"

"The truth about what?" Mr. Ketchum asked, seemingly confused.

"Why you always kept me away from other kids. Why I could always get straight A's without trying. The truth about my being a scanner!"

The sound of the word "scanner" brought a tense silence to the room. Susan Ketchum started to speak and then turned away, catching her thoughts in her throat.

"You *know* what the word means, don't you?" David pressed, raising his voice, demanding a response.

This time, it was his father's turn to move away. Rising from his chair, he moved across the room to join his wife of forty years. They looked at each other in silence as if each was waiting for the other to speak.

Susan Ketchum finally turned to face her son. Fussing with her hair that was pulled back in a bun secured with several barrettes, she was the picture of tormented guilt. "You were always such a special boy, David," she began.

George Ketchum moved in front of his wife, stopping her in midsentence. Sitting back down next to the bed, he took his son's hand in his own and confessed. "David, we're not your real parents, your mother and I."

David was stunned. He was prepared to accept the fact that he was a scanner, but never had it dawned on him that he wasn't the Ketchums' own flesh and blood. He searched his father's eyes for an explanation. His mother began to weep softly across the room.

"You mean I'm adopted," David asked incredulously.

"Eventually, we adopted you, yes," Mr. Ketchum added gently, still rubbing his son's hand.

"I don't understand. If you're not my real parents, then who are they?"

Once again there was silence. The memories of the past were difficult sins to bring into the present.

"Your mother's name was Kim Oberist. Your father was a man named Cameron Vale. They're both dead," George Ketchum said, quickly adding, "No one really knows what happened. They died when you were still a baby."

David was more alarmed now than ever. The truth of his life was finally beginning to become clear. "You mean that my parents . . . they were scanners, too?"

"They used that word," Mr. Ketchum admitted. "It took us a long time to realize what it meant."

David felt like screaming. He somehow felt betrayed by the only people that were his life. He threw back the bedcovers and rose to walk across the room. Back and forth he paced without speaking, trying to absorb the impact of what he had just heard.

"Your parents never wanted to give you up," Mr. Ketchum continued. "You've got to believe they loved you as much as we do. In fact, they loved you so much that they brought you to us to watch over you for a few months, they said. They told us that their lives were in danger and they wanted to keep you safe. Obviously, they had good reason to fear."

Mrs. Ketchum placed her arm around David's shoulders, trying to console her son as he mourned the parents he never knew. "David. Your parents were fine, fine people. But you know how much we've always loved you, too."

It was more than David could bear to hear. He struggled to escape his mother's grasp, tossing her free of his shoulders and releasing his pent-up emotion. Tears welled up in his eyes; he grabbed his jacket and silently left the room.

David needed to walk, to think, to sort things out in his mind. It seemed in the last few days his entire life had been turned inside out. Nothing was as he thought it was, no one whom he thought they were.

As he walked past the old barn around the pumphouse and through the meadow, he longed for the old days when he felt so protected that nothing could hurt him except loneliness. So much had changed since then.

Breathing the pristine air deep into his lungs, David

hiked through the woods, at one with nature, thrilling to every sound he heard. The birds seemed to sense his sadness, he thought, and trilled a special rhapsody to cheer him up. In the distance, he noticed several deer crossing high on a hill, their sleek bodies moving quickly as they caught his scent.

Pausing to sit upon a rock, David gazed down upon the verdant valley below, working slowly through his situation. He wanted to be normal; he wanted to have a normal life. But such was the stuff of dreams, and his life had become a recurring nightmare.

As he lay on the lush grass, he felt its cool moisture dampening his shirt. He loved the sensation of the wind blowing across his chest and through his hair. It was the perfect elixir to drift him to sleep.

In their living room, the Ketchums were a study in confusion. They had done their best to protect David, to care for him, to love him. Now, his world was falling apart and theirs with it.

George Ketchum decided as he looked at the sadness in his wife's face that whatever it took, whatever he had to do, he would make her smile again. Surely a quiet talk with David would straighten things out, make them right again. David had to be made to understand that what had happened to him was not of their doing.

Walking out on the front porch, George called for his son, but to no avail. Walking around behind the house, he found no trace of the confused boy he had raised. The barn was empty as well. Only his battered truck remained as proof of his visit. Well, at least, George thought, he could do something about that.

He had just finished pulling David's truck into the barn and was sliding the heavy door closed when he noticed a car coming up the dirt road in his direction at top speed, a trail of dust spanning out behind it. It was a late model Ford, pulling up to the house.

Mrs. Ketchum heard the car's engine and came out on the front porch, curious about the visitors. Her husband waved her frantically inside.

As Ketchum cautiously approached the car, a large man with a crewcut slid from the driver's seat and put out his hand in greeting. Another, more slender, man stayed in the car.

"Hello. My name's Gelson," he said, shaking George Ketchum's hand. "I'm a friend of your son, David. Is he around?"

The man had a strange air about him, Ketchum thought. A little too friendly, a little too nosy, for his own good. He was definitely trouble.

"No . . . No, he isn't," George Ketchum lied, looking the man straight in the eyes.

"Well, when do you expect him back?" Gelson countered.

"Oh, probably sometime around Christmas, I figure," David's father replied, trying his best to look casual and at ease.

From the front door, Mrs. Ketchum viewed her husband and the strangers with foreboding. She too sensed danger.

"You must think I'm pretty stupid, old man," Gelson said, suddenly turning cold and sharp.

He turned toward Mrs. Ketchum at the front of the house. Moving to protect his wife and his property, Ketchum blocked his path. "I'm afraid you and your friend are going to have to leave," he said firmly, leaving no doubt that he meant business.

Though up in years, Ketchum was still a strong and virile man. His years of working on the farm had seen to that. And he wasn't about to let a pair of strangers invade the sanctity of his home.

After a tense momentary stand-off, Gelson seemed to back away. "Sure, sure," he said as he shot a look at Drak, still seated in the car.

As Drak slowly opened the door, Ketchum continued to hold his ground. "This is private property, and I've asked you to leave it," he stated with authority.

"I understand," Lieutenant Gelson replied, smiling briefly at Drak.

Fearing now for his wife's safety, Ketchum walked quickly back to the house as Gelson and Drak watched his every move. Ushering her inside, Ketchum tried not to show his fear.

"Who are they, George?" she whispered, looking out the front curtain.

"They're looking for David," Ketchum answered, not knowing what else they were after.

"They're coming this way, George!" Susan Ketchum said hysterically, quickly dropping the curtain back in place.

"Go upstairs and call Sheriff Johnson. Hurry!" he instructed her. He walked to the wall and pulled down his 12-gauge shotgun from its rack. He heard the intruders walk up on the wooden front porch and turned to face them.

Without warning, Drak kicked in the front door, splintering the frame and sending pieces of glass flying into the living room. From upstairs, Mrs. Ketchum stifled a scream as she waited for the sheriff to come on the line.

"I thought I told you to leave," Ketchum demanded.

"And now we're telling *you*, Mr. Ketchum," Lieutenant Gelson shouted back.

Quickly, George Ketchum leveled his shotgun to take aim. But before his finger could hit the trigger, Drak scanned him and sent him reeling backward across the room into the Victorian bookcase against the wall.

"Upstairs!" Gelson snapped at Drak, who immediately began taking the steps two at a time.

Though Ketchum was dazed, he managed to roll over and get off one shotgun blast. Without time to aim, he merely grazed Gelson's arm, causing no damage.

Cursing, Gelson kicked the shotgun out of Ketchum's hand, drawing his pistol in anger.

"Susan," Ketchum managed to yell, then a shot from the pistol hit him squarely in the chest, the blast's force flattening him to the floor.

Hearing the gunshot from her bedroom upstairs, Mrs. Ketchum turned to find Drak standing at the door.

He motioned to the receiver in her hand. "Drop it!" he shouted, barely audible over her scream. "Drop it or you're dead."

Susan Ketchum was frozen in place. She couldn't speak, she couldn't even move as she heard the sheriff's dispatcher on the line. Ripping the phone from her hand and slamming her down on the bed with a blow to the chest, Drak put the receiver to his ear and heard the dispatcher clearly now.

"Hello, hello. Mrs. Ketchum?"

Drak sneered icily, pulling his gun from his shoulder holster; he aimed it at close range at Susan Ketchum before speaking. "Sorry, but she can't talk right now," he said, and then coldbloodedly fired his gun at Mrs. Ketchum's head before hanging up the phone.

The sound of a shotgun blast wakened David with a start. A chill raced through his body as he leapt to his feet and began charging through the woods toward the farmhouse. His heart was pounding home the urgency of his mission as he pushed himself through rugged trails, stumbling only once over a hidden tree stump.

Reversing the path he had taken earlier, he raced past the pumphouse, taking a shortcut through the barn, dashing around its bales of hay, out into the clearing just in time to see a car tearing down the dirt road toward the main highway.

David feared the worst. His adrenaline was pumping as he charged across the lawn and onto the front porch, shocked to see the old door smashed off its hinges. Even more shocking was what he saw inside.

His father was slowly pulling himself across the floor, leaving a trail of blood across the rag rug and out into the hallway.

"Dad!" David yelled, rushing to his side. Cradling his father's head in his arms with tears streaming down his face, David could hardly see and couldn't talk. The sight of his father lying mortally injured, his chest ripped open, his organs exposed, was more than he could bear.

"Upstairs," his father gasped. "Help her!"

Again, David's blood ran cold. "Not Mom. Dear God, not Mom," he screamed as he gently laid his father's head on his rolled up jacket and bounded up the steps.

David instinctively called out to his mother as he ran from room to room searching for her. When he opened the master bedroom door, he was stunned. Never had he seen anything so shocking.

His mother was stretched across the bed, her eyes wide open in fear. The lower right side of her jaw had been blown away by a bullet shot at close range. Black powder burns ringed her cheek. The chenille bedspread was soaked in the blood that had drained from the back of her head down along her body.

Knowing she was dead, not wanting to see more, he backed away from the body of his brutally murdered mother. His expression was numb as he headed toward the stairs. His father was clinging to the bottom step and bannister. From the look on David's face, his father knew his wife was dead. He slowly rolled his eyes toward the back of his head and slumped against the stairs.

David staggered down the steps, slowly, deliberately, shocked into the reality of the moment. He had to call for help, yet his body wasn't responding to his brain's plea for speed. As he crouched down by his father's head once again, he pleaded for the wounded man to wake up.

In the far distance, he heard the faintest sound of a siren heading his way. Leaving his father's side, he raced out across the front porch down the dirt road waving his arms frantically.

The ambulance which met him midway along the road had been sent by the sheriff's dispatcher in response to Susan Ketchum's call. The small town paramedics were not prepared for what they saw when they entered the farmhouse they knew so well.

They couldn't wait for the sheriff to arrive on the scene. While David's mother was obviously beyond reviving, George Ketchum needed their help now. They immediately began to administer oxygen and injected him with a drug to stabilize his heart.

He had lost major amounts of blood and needed to be rushed to the hospital immediately. David's father was gently lifted and strapped on his back to the gurney. Hating to leave his mother, but knowing that his father needed him desperately now, David joined the paramedic in the back of the ambulance as it headed toward the emergency room.

As he crouched next to father, he scanned him gently to stir his mind into consciousness. Half-waking, semicomatose, the weak old man looked into his son's eyes, unable to speak.

"You're going to be okay, Dad," David whispered quietly to his father, his voice barely audible over the siren's wail.

David's father just shook his head, a tear gently running down his cheek. He didn't want to live anymore. Not without Susan.

Reading his father's mind, David put his arm around his bandaged chest. "No, I won't let you go. You're all I have now. Promise me, Father."

The wounded man responded without speaking, knowing full well that David's scanning was picking up his thoughts. "Your mother was my life." With that, his eyes closed as if in sleep.

"Dad! Stay awake," David insisted, shaking his father gently. "I know how much you loved her. But you can't give up. You can't die now. I need you. You're all I have left," he repeated.

Slowly lifting his eyelids, George Ketchum made a decision. If he was dying, David should know anyway. He hadn't any right to keep a secret now. "*No, David. You have someone else.*"

Picking up his thought-waves, David looked perplexed. "Someone else?" he asked. "What?"

"*An older sister,*" Ketchum's inner voice revealed. "*Her name is Julie and she lives up north. Lake Washimeska.*" Then he closed his eyes once more.

David was stunned. *A sister*? He had a sister all these years and no one had told him. His reaction was a mixture of anger and joy. He couldn't believe the news, but he hoped that his father was right.

Scanning him with controlled force, David directed his father's body to respond, to begin the healing process in earnest. Slowly, the life-support monitors reflected an improvement in Ketchum's condition.

"He's coming back . . . I don't believe it," the paramedic stared incredulously at the blips on the machine.

As David caressed his father's brow and continued his healing scan, his only thoughts were of his father's total recovery—and of a sister he had never known.

CHAPTER SEVEN

JULIE

"*Dear Julie,*" began the inscription in her high school yearbook. "*Knowing you these past few years has made my life complete. Only you can realize how your encouragement and understanding has allowed me to tolerate an impossible situation. I will always love you and need you by my side. Walter.*"

Almost illegible in appearance, the inscription was scrawled across the page, ending just to the left of the picture of a rather pleasant-looking teenager with long blonde hair hanging limply on either side of her face. Though there was a slight smile on her lips, her eyes had the look of a young girl who had endured extensive pain and suffering.

The words running underneath the photograph identified the girl as "*JULIE MARIE VALE, Hempsted, Vermont.*" Her biography said she was a member of Latin Club I and II, and the Junior League. "*The most clairvoyant,*" the paragraph ended. Three lines, no more, to describe an entire life.

The yearbook failed to mention that—and indeed no one in Lynnewood High even realized—Julie Marie Vale was a scanner. The daughter of scanners Cameron Vale and Kim Oberist, she was dedicated to preserving their memory by remaining alive despite the odds in a country which treated scanners like a contagious illness—something that needed to be stamped out at all costs.

As a child she came to know the danger of living with powers so special that men would kill to silence them. Early on she learned her world would always be one of secrecy and fear. An existence marred by an accident of heredity.

After her parents gave her up for adoption, she lived in the hills far from the crowds and restrictions of civilized man. Developing her skills at wilderness survival, she became a loner capable of existing for days in the woods.

Her best friends became the creatures of nature, who, like her, were being hunted into virtual extinction. Always in fear of discovery. Always poised for attack or retreat.

Julie Marie Vale, Hempsted, Vermont.

David spent that night and the next in a small Vermont hospital keeping a vigilant watch over his father. The old man had several setbacks during the first few hours, mainly due to the large amount of blood he had lost.

By the end of the second night, however, the doctors

on duty were labeling his recovery "miraculous"; and when it became apparent that the crisis was over, David knew it was time to leave and follow through on the promise he had made at the farmhouse: to catch those responsible for his mother's brutal murder and kill them himself.

Since that day on the farm, his entire being had been possessed by an all-encompassing desire to strike back at the forces that had turned his life into a maelstrom of hatred and bloodshed. It seemed to track him everywhere; if he was to ever regain his sense of self and well-being, he knew that he had to act, and act quickly, before he too was destroyed.

It was ironic that his feelings for Alice had taken a backseat to revenge; that was what bothered David the most about his obsessive drive to even the score. Alice was the most innocent pawn of all in this bizarre plot in which he was a principle player. He knew he must protect her, even if it meant never seeing her again.

While his truck's windshield was being replaced on the outskirts of town in a tiny garage run by his childhood friend, burly, dark-haired "Big" Dave Mindak, David debated whether to call Alice and update her on the tragic events of the past few days. There was little to say that made sense to him, so violent was the attack against his parents, so unprovoked an assault on a defenseless couple. Yet, he knew Alice would want to know that he was safe. He owed her that much, at least.

When the phone rang in Alice's kitchen, she had been outside watching the police car across the street. Off and on for the past few days, she had noticed various patrol cars parked in her neighborhood, and now she began to realize why. She was under surveillance, like a criminal being stalked for capture.

She realized, of course, that it was David the police were after. She also knew that she might be their only link to the man she loved.

At the first ring of the telephone, Alice jumped instinctively and rushed through the back door to grab the receiver. "David," she said, her voice full of hope.

"I've only got a second to talk," he answered, aware that her phone might be tapped.

"David, don't say anything. The police. They're watching me . . . looking for you!"

Feeling the tears welling up again, David blurted out the truth that he couldn't deny. "They killed my mother."

"Oh my God!"

"I just wanted to make sure you're safe. They're probably listening. I have to go."

Choking back tears, Alice held the receiver close to her mouth and whispered, "David. I love you."

"I love you too," David answered as he hung up the line, sure of himself and full of warm emotion.

Alice stared at the phone for a long minute, the dial tone blaring into the air. "I love you, David," she repeated to herself, wondering how the horror attacking their life together would ever be replaced by happiness.

The past few days had brought intense scrutiny and public recognition for the new police commissioner. Forrester was enjoying himself and his celebrity as he had at no other time in his life. He loved the attention; he even enjoyed the skepticism that surrounded his appointment.

He had purchased several new suits, appropriate additions to the wardrobe of a police commissioner, he felt. In fact, he was wearing one now as the television cameras were once again setting up in his office—the third time they had done so in the past two days.

They had been dogging him during the course of his day, trying to learn more about his controversial new order and what it would mean to the crime element in the city. Without support from the mayor, the plan would be difficult to implement, Forrester knew. But there had been rumors circulating about the mayor's capabilities. Rumors he knew well, since he had started them all.

"Just one more question, Commissioner Forrester," news anchor Carrie Olson was asking as her crew followed the police executive toward his office.

"Make it fast," he answered, realizing he was late for his next interview.

"Lately, you've been putting yourself more and more in the public eye. Clearly, you've become an outspoken advocate of change in our city," Olson stated.

Forrester stopped at his office door, making no effort to hide his frustration. "Get to the question, Ms. Olson and quickly."

"Well, sir, would it be fair to assume that you're considering running for mayor?" she said, obviously intimidated by the new commissioner.

Pausing for what he thought would be an appropriate time, Forrester went into an act he had rehearsed for several days. He knew the question would arise, just as he knew his answer had to be phrased very carefully.

"The voters are looking for someone to keep the city under control," he said. "So, if the people need me, *yes*, I'll run."

As David's truck bumped along the dirt road bordered by a large forest of maple trees, he felt a nervous knot beginning to grow in his stomach. Frankly, he was worried.

After twenty-five years, how could he simply walk into the life of a woman he didn't remember and think of her as his sister? Perhaps even more important, how could he tell her about his adoptive mother's murder, and the scores of police hunting him down?

His father hadn't told him much more about her than the fact that she lived, all alone, in a very remote part of the state. He glanced down at the roughly drawn map his father had given him in the hospital, which pointed the way to Julie Vale's cabin.

With the road getting rougher with each increasing mile and his stomach bouncing around with the bumps, David silently hoped his journey would be over soon. The area was beautiful enough. Stands of maple blossomed thick with green leaves on each side of the road, a chorus of birds singing from each treetop.

It was an especially sunny day, David thought as he drove out of the trees into a wide clearing, the glare bouncing off the hood of his truck. In the distance, he saw what must be Julie's log cabin, a mud-caked old jeep parked beside it, and cords of wood piled high on the cabin's other side.

David pulled his truck alongside the jeep and stepped out of the cab; only the haunting call of a loon interrupted the tranquility of the setting. Overcome with emotion, he approached the primitive rustic shelter, more a wilderness sanctuary than a home.

The cabin, built on a rise overlooking the valley below, and its setting were picture-book perfect. The kind of place where one imagined a fire burning every night, with family huddled around wrapped in comforters. Warm, friendly, basic.

David walked up to the door, his heart pounding in anticipation; he knocked and waited. He knocked again; still no response. Trying the doorknob, he found that it was unlocked, presenting yet another decision.

Wanting to enter yet afraid that he shouldn't, David

stood frozen in place trying to decide what to do. Finally gaining the courage, he pushed the door wide to reveal a small, well-kept living room.

The sunlight splintered itself through the spaces between the logs as much as through the dirty window, slicing beams of brightness in the darkened room. In the corner, smoke rose from a potbellied stove. How long it had been since he had seen one of those, David thought.

The few pieces of furniture were well-worn, but comfortable. The sofa especially looked inviting with its caftan thrown across the back.

Bookshelves lined two entire walls; his sister must love to read, David realized. It was a trait they both shared. As David moved toward shelves he wasn't as captivated by the book titles as he was by the photographs on each shelf.

There was a common female in each. Julie, he thought. She was coupled in several with someone who was obviously a boyfriend, or perhaps her husband. Their eyes shared that special magic of love.

A snapshot of a young couple holding a baby caught his attention as he was about to turn and leave. Reaching up for a closer look, David suddenly felt the presence of someone else in the room. Spinning quickly, he was surprised to see a woman silhouetted in the doorway.

She wore patched overalls over her small frame; her checkered shirt was equally as worn and repaired. Her long blonde hair was simply yet elegantly mounded on top of her head, and pinned in place. Her beauty radiated, despite her rough exterior.

"God, you look so much like Father," she said, after several seconds of silence. "My name is Julie Vale."

David ran across the cabin to hug the sister he had never known existed—his link to a past he did not know. "I'm David," he said. "David, your brother."

She nodded in love and excitement; their eyes held each other, sharing the joy of being reunited. Suddenly, Julie's expression deepened as she felt the pain of David's experiences.

She quietly led him to a seat before asking what had happened. As he related the events of the past several days, he saw the sadness in her eyes radiating a beauty different from that of her face. Her caring was deep and true, David knew. At last, he had found someone who understood.

"When I left the hospital, he was going to be just fine," David finished his story. "Then I came here," he added, stopping to choke back his tears of rage and fear. "What do they want from me," he pleaded, hoping the Julie would have the answer.

"To control you," she said softly. "To use you. It's that simple. And they will, if you allow them to."

"But people aren't things, tools to be used and broken . . ." David reasoned.

"To them you are. Everybody is," Julie replied. Touching his hand and placing it in her own, she knew what she had to tell him would not be easy. Her story of sadness rivaled his own, yet it had been going on far longer. "It was the same with Mom and Dad. Your real Mom and Dad," she said softly, staring deeply into his eyes in an attempt to rivet out the grief. "They were talking to other scanners, bringing them together, discussing what they should do with their powers. But some people wanted to use them then, just like they want to use you now."

David began to speak, but Julie silenced him and continued. "David, listen. Mom and Dad wanted no part of being used. They opposed everyone that would take advantage of their special gifts. So they were killed." Julie drifted off in silence, drawing deep into her memories of precious moments past.

David wanted to ask more about his real parents, but he sensed the pain it would cause Julie to recall the years when their parents were still living. Still, he had to know why they gave him up. Why him and not her?

"Mom and Dad knew that by refusing to cooperate, they would be placing their very lives in danger. I would hear them late at night discussing plans to get out of town with other scanners who would secretly meet at our house. The kind of things they discussed would scare me so that I couldn't sleep," Julie confessed.

She rose from the sofa and walked over to the potbellied stove, stirring the coal embers with a stoking rod. "One day, they came to me and said you were going to live with the Ketchums. You were only three or four then. So very young."

"And you. What about you?" David asked.

"They sent me away, too. To live with some people in the hills not far away from here. They died about eight years ago—first the husband, and several months later, his wife," Julie revealed. "The people who killed Mom and Dad don't ever give up. Our special gift won't let them. That's why I came up here to live, eight years ago. And I'll never go back."

"Aren't you lonely, living here all alone."

Reluctantly Julie answered, not sure how much she should reveal. "I had a boyfriend back there. My *fiancé*, Walter," she said, smiling at the old-fashioned delicacy of the word.

Suddenly, feeling a familiar tingle in her temples, she turned to face David directly. "Don't!" she screamed in anger. "Don't you dare try to scan me, David. If you want to know something, ask, and I'll tell you. At least give me that much respect."

Julie's unexpected rage startled David, leaving him trying to make excuses when there were none to be found. "I didn't mean . . . I'm sorry," he blurted forth, unable to think up anything clever to say.

"Yes, Walter was a scanner," Julie snapped. "Isn't that what you wanted to know. Yes, we were both scanners, David."

"Julie, please," David said apologetically. "I only wanted to know because I wanted to know what it was like, well, being with another scanner. Was that . . ."

"It was easier in a way," she said, remembering life with Walter in another time, another place. "Things you didn't have to explain. Things you never had to say. Unfortunately, Walter didn't understand his power. He worried about its effect on people and how it could best be used."

Those words hit David especially hard, echoing in his mind.

"He decided to enter a program and they gave him a drug."

"EPH-2," David shot back.

"No, back then it was EPH-1. Remember, we're talking about eight years ago. Morse, the doctor . . ."

"Dr. Morse. I know Dr. Morse. And Forrester?" David questioned.

"Forrester is the one who killed Dad."

David reacted with the stunned expression of one who has been jolted by electricity—disbelief coupled with residual side effects.

"Forrester killed my real father?" he repeated incredulously. He wanted to scream in rage; only his reason kept him calm and listening.

"I tried my best to get Walter away," Julie continued. "But he wouldn't listen. At first, he seemed to know exactly what he was doing. At times, he even seemed to be enjoying himself. Before I could stop him, he was addicted. Behaving strangely, and worse, doing some awful things.''

David's heart was breaking as he listened to Julie relate a saga he knew too well. Drak's story of addicted scanners in holding tanks in the basement of the institute made more sense now.

"One day, he disappeared," she added. "And the cops came after me. I had to kill two of them," she shrugged, almost stoically.

David was nearly hysterical at the news that his sister, too, had killed. This business of scanners was like a giant wheel, rolling and rolling to absolutely nowhere. "This has got to end. Somebody has got to stop them."

With bitter resignation, Julie simply shook her head. "Don't even try, David. They're animals. Let them destroy each other, not you."

David was on his feet. He didn't care that Julie thought it was hopeless. It didn't matter that he was one against many. If he didn't try to save himself and others, he would never be able to live anyway.

He walked to the door, then he turned to Julie, who was rising from the sofa. "I love a girl back there," David admitted.

"A normal?" Julie asked. Not waiting for an answer she knew all too well, she sighed understandingly. "You poor boy. It will never work. I know. I've tried."

"And I have to try, too," David insisted, walking toward his truck. "There's got to be a way, and I'll find it if I have to scan every person in Vermont."

As David pulled himself in the cab of his truck, he turned to wave goodbye to his sister. Framed by the log cabin, she stood in simple elegance on the front porch.

"David," she mouthed in his direction.

Looking at her eyes, he nodded, knowing exactly what she wanted to say. The love in her heart engulfed his soul. Smiling, he said, "Me, too. I do, too." Then, he started his engine and slowly headed down the dirt road home.

CHAPTER EIGHT
MAYOR FRANZONI

The only thing in the small envelope David received from Julie was a yellowed newspaper clipping. In fact, at first, he thought the photograph at the top of the article was Julie, herself.

The heading under the photograph read: *"Kim Oberist Vale, dead at thirty-four."* It was his mother's obituary notice, lovingly saved all these years by Julie. He parked under a large shade tree near a swiftly flowing stream and quietly absorbed the clipping's contents.

"Kim Oberist Vale, activist and poet, has died at the age of 34.

Vale died Monday night at Saint Mary Hospital in Landford, according to the Holmby & McEverett Funeral Home. The cause of death was not released.

Vale was a well-known local poet with several books to her credit, including Songs My Mother Taught Me *and* When Elephants and Flamingos First Join Hands. *One of her poems was read to Congress by Rep. Harold Grenville (D-Vt.) during his effort to introduce a bill forbidding the advance testing of experimental drugs on humans.*

Vale was married to activist Cameron Vale, who died under mysterious circumstances last September. The pair were familiar fixtures at sit-ins at the Biocarbon Amalgamate headquarters where testing of experimental drugs is reported to be widespread. It was during one such sit-in that Vale's husband was taken into custody by security guards and not heard from again.

Under the name Darryl Revok, her husband was once in charge of Biocarbon Amalgamate's testing and production program. His body was recovered several months later in Fort Worth, Texas. He apparently committed suicide, and his body was so badly decomposed that the local coroner refused to assign a cause of death.

After her husband's death, Vale lived in virtual seclusion in the hills above Lake Winnipesaukee, and was thought to be writing another book of poetry.

She was born Kimberly Joan Oberist in Gleasondale, Massachusetts, and was credited with having clairvoyant abilities as a young child, performing in Boston on WBZ-TV's "Stars of Tomorrow" show as well as at county fairs throughout the state.

Survivors are believed to include a daughter and a son, both of whom were placed in adoption.

In her will, Vale asked that donations be made to

Women Against Drugs, New York, New York. No services are planned.

The long drive back to the city found David without a clear plan of action. Direct attack seemed out of the question. He was only one and they were many. He was an easy target and an easy victim.

If he had any hope of eliminating the genocide that continued to occur at the institute, he needed clout more than muscle, the kind of clout that only a political figure could muster.

The beautiful Vermont countryside seemed strangely at odds with his task ahead. The trees, lush with the foliage of spring, seemed particularly abundant and full of vitality, contrary to the life-draining scanners like Drak and Feck and the men who supplied them with addicting drugs like EPH-2.

Introspective, confused, and sad beyond his comprehension, David nevertheless remained steadfast in his goal to succeed where others had failed. Obviously, any call for police intervention would meet with a swift and violent reaction. Forrester and Gelson would see to that. No, only a fullscale investigation by the state itself would stand any chance of success.

As his mind raced with alternative scenarios, one name continually surfaced—Mayor Franzoni. After all, it was the mayor who witnessed the power of scanners firsthand when she unexpectedly announced Wayne Forrester as her new commissioner of police, and left the podium, without explanation, a touch of blood on her nostril. Yes, David thought, Mayor Franzoni must be convinced to act, and act now, to stop what would otherwise mean disaster for the state and eventually the country.

As he crossed the state line and headed toward the city,

David felt a sudden calm begin to give his body and mind a renewed strength. Though he realized that it would not be simple to convince the mayor that there were people in her jurisdiction that could take control of her mind through telepathy, he also realized he had the power in his own mind to prove the point beyond any doubt.

Almost smiling now, he turned on the radio, hoping to relax as he drove the final minutes to City Hall. Ironically, instead of soothing music, he happened upon an afternoon news report. The announcer's bombshell chilled his very soul.

"Apparently disenchanted with what he calls, 'Mayor Franzoni's dismal failure to halt crime in our city,' acting Police Commissioner Wayne Forrester has announced his intention to challenge the mayor in the upcoming election."

It was as if Forrester has somehow read his mind and knew his plan, and was intent on removing the one person who might be able to stop this insanity from continuing.

"Furthermore," the announcer continued, "a New Radio Insta-Poll has revealed that of one hundred sampled voters, *more than half* would vote for Commissioner Forrester if the election were held today."

From her bedroom radio, Alice was hearing the same broadcast. She, too, realized the drastic implications of Forrester's plan to take over the city government. Like a slow and infectious cancer, Forrester's deadly expansion of power would surely mean success for his new order and death for hundreds, if not thousands, of people.

Quickly tossing a heavy sweatshirt over her T-shirt and grabbing her purse, Alice headed out the door, unsure of where she was going but knowing well she had to do something.

"Sorry, Miss Leonardo. But orders are to keep you here until this little matter is cleared up," directed an officer standing outside, raising his arm to block her path. His badge said his name was Carver.

Stunned into the realization that she was not only being watched, but was now a prisoner in her own home, Alice just shook her head in disbelief. "What . . . ?" she asked, almost in a trance.

"If there's anything you need . . . anything we can get you, just let us know," Officer Carver stated, leading her back into the house.

Oh, David, where are you? she thought as she lay back down on her bed, feeling more helpless now than ever, not even knowing whether he was alive or dead.

In his office inside City Hall, acting Police Commissioner Forrester was smiling as he, too, heard the news report. "I'm going to win this election, Guy," he said to Lieutenant Gelson seated nearby with his feet up on Forrester's desk.

"No doubt, sir," Gelson replied, frantically drawing on a cigar he was attempting to light.

"You know what that means, don't you," Forrester said as he rose and slammed Gelson's feet to the floor.

Gelson was coughing now, exhaling a gush of smoke from his lungs as he gasped for air. "What, sir?" he wheezed in between spasms.

"That *you* are going to be the next commissioner of police," Forrester replied, removing Gelson's cigar and stubbing out the stogie in a large ashtray on his desk. "But only if you find David Ketchum." Suddenly, Forrester's smile was gone. "I don't care if you have to use every man in this department. Just bring him back—dead or alive. It no longer matters."

Gelson looked like a smiling Cheshire cat as he gently removed his crushed cigar from the ashtray, attempted to straighten out the end as best he could, and placed it gingerly in his jacket pocket. "Funny you should mention him, sir," Gelson laughed in Forrester's direction. "We spotted him, and he's parked right outside City Hall."

"You idiot," Forrester blasted. "You're sitting here and he's out front?"

Forrester picked up his ashtray and aimed it in Gelson's direction, but the lieutenant was already out the door.

David Ketchum had been patient. He had waited silently on a side street next to City Hall, strategically located right across from the garage which housed Mayor Franzoni's limousine. He knew full well that charging into the mayor's office with stories about scanners would only get him thrown in jail—or worse.

The mayor's limousine was another story. And David's patience was about to pay off. From his position crouched down low in the cab of his truck, he saw the long, black Lincoln Continental creep out of the garage, the mayor barely visible behind the tinted black glass.

He started his truck's engine, and after waiting until the limo turned widely at the corner, proceeded to follow at a discreet distance. Through the downtown area, past office buildings whose doorways were the temporary shelters of the homeless, along the manicured avenues of the shopping district, and into the area's wealthiest section, David kept pace, never losing sight of the limousine.

At the far corner, David saw the car pull through the wrought-iron gates of an English Tudor estate. The eight-foot-high eugenia hedge which surrounded the property blocked most of the view from the street, but the enormity of the house itself was evident by the eight large chimneys that towered over all. As the electronic gates began to swing slowly closed, David pulled his pickup near the curb, silently contemplating his next move.

With the movement of a cat burglar, David slid out from behind the steering wheel and slipped inside the property just as the gates crashed shut. Walking swiftly up the driveway, with visions of Doberman pinschers about to bound forth from some hidden observation point, David approached the front door with trepidation.

Mayor Franzoni's desk sat in plain view of an enormous bay-window, that was elaborately designed with leaded and stained glass. Hued in the multicolor reflections of the sun streaming through the window, the mayor was playing her role as chief executive of a metropolitan city to the hilt as she spoke on the telephone.

"Listen to me, Monsignor. There will be no benefit for the convent unless I authorize a benefit for the convent. And I'm not authorizing anything until I receive word from the cardinal himself." She paused, clicking her ruby-red fingernail on the mahogany desktop. "Oh, so now he does have the time to call me. I'm so pleased." Another pause. "I'll expect his call."

As she hung up there was a certain look that crossed her face. Not a smile, but more the satisfied look of a tigress that has just finished ripping apart a hyena. As she contemplated her victory, her office door opened.

"Pardon me, ma'am," a tuxedoed butler said with a slight bow. "But there is a gentlemen here to speak to you." The butler's speech was slow and deliberate; the look of someone whose behavior was driven by a scan. "It's about Commissioner Forrester. He says it's very important."

"I am not expecting a caller, Henry," she snapped back. "Tell him he'll have to make an appointment like everyone else."

The mayor barely had mouthed the end of the sentence when David barged into the room, commanding the butler to leave with a look from his eyes.

"Now just a minute, young man," Mayor Franzoni said, standing behind her desk unintimidated. "Just who are you and what the hell do you think you're doing!"

"Please, just sit down and listen," David begged, hoping she wasn't already pressing some sort of silent alarm.

The mayor didn't speak; nor did she sit. She merely continued to glare at her uninvited guest with open hostility.

"My name is David Ketchum, and I know you didn't mean to appoint Forrester to the post of police commissioner."

"And how would you know that, David Ketchum," she said sarcastically. Intrigued by her own little game of words, she sat down gracefully, never letting her eyes leave his.

"Because I made you do it."

A shrill little laugh left the mayor's lips, coupled with a roll of her heavily mascaraed eyes. "You made me?" she joked in disbelief. "And how, exactly, did you do that?" she asked.

"I was born with a kind of telepathic ability. I used it on you," David said, knowing full well she wasn't believing him. "There are others like me. Some of us have been forced to work for Forrester. They call us scanners."

Mayor Franzoni was beginning to tire of this game. "Scanners. Excuse me, Mr. Ketchum. I'm really not amused," she said curtly. "Scanners," she repeated. "Don't make me laugh—"

David's scan cut her off in midsentence. Enough explanation; it was now time for a demonstration.

"Don't make you laugh, Mayor?" David mocked. "I can make you laugh or cry. I can make you do anything."

Mayor Franzoni continued to stare, caught in David's scan and unable to move. Held in the grip of a scanner against her will, she was discovering his message firsthand.

David pointed to the cigarette box on her desk. "Light a cigarette," he demanded.

"I don't smoke," she insisted, unmoving. "Those are just for . . ."

As David concentrated harder, the mayor tried to finish her sentence. She opened her mouth to speak, but no words came forth, no sounds were uttered. Against her will, she found herself opening the cigarette box and reaching for a lighter. Taking a cigarette in her left hand, she placed it to her mouth and lit it, visibly trembling.

His demonstration a success, his purpose completed, he released the mayor from his grip. The taste of tobacco edged into her mouth, a constant reminder that he had done what he had promised.

"Tell me more about this," the mayor said, as she returned to her seat, obviously impressed.

"It is done solely with the power of the mind," he answered, moving closer to the desk. "It is a power we scanners are born with, a result of the drug Ephemerol on the fetus. In some people, the power can be developed and nourished. It's like honing a skill," David explained. "Yet in the wrong hands, it can be disastrous. Using scanners, Forrester can control anyone he wants. Unless we stop him now . . ."

It wasn't until the mayor punched several numbers into the phone on her desk that David fully realized she believed him.

"This is Mayor Franzoni. I need to speak with the assistant director right now. Tell him I . . ." Those were to be her final words.

As David stood in front of her, a rifle shot rang out. He watched as a bullet smashed through the leaded glass window and struck the mayor on the back of the head, then exploded out the frontal lobe, killing her instantly.

Her body fell forward, smashing on the desk and splattering David with a blood. "No!" he cried, rushing to her aid, helpless to stop the life fluid from draining out of her body.

David ran to the window and saw the back of a man escaping over the exterior wall. Screaming for help, he raced to the office door, only to be met by the butler who reacted in horror at the sight before him.

"Get out of my way," David shouted at the man, who was frozen in fear by the horror of death. Pushing past the butler, David charged down the hallway toward the front door, across the glazed marble floor entry just as two uniformed S.W.A.T. team members bolted through the entrance, each armed with sniperscoped rifles.

"Stop. Police," one yelled as David turned in desperation. "Stop or we'll shoot," he heard as he ran down the opposite corridor, uncertain where it would lead.

He rounded the corner, as a bullet ricocheted past his skull. The sound of rifle shots echoed in his head; bullets tore at the plaster from the walls. Through the kitchen and out the side door he ran, escape being his only motive.

Making a sprint across the lawn toward the hedged wall, David could hear the sound of more patrol cars surrounding the property and penning him inside. The piercing sound of their sirens drummed through his head like minibullets.

David turned in retreat, realizing that escape without confrontation was now impossible. Even as he headed back toward the kitchen, two additional police rounded the corner, their submachine guns ready to fire.

Standing his ground, David prepared for battle, turning on a scan to save his life and those of innocents in the city. "All right, you bastards," he said, summoning up his power to massive momentum, snapping his head and concentrating with all his might.

His scan hit the two patrolman with enough force to rip the weapons from their grasp, throw them backward, and smash them into the brick wall of the house. With the pair out of commission, David turned his energy back to escaping, hoping to reach the back wall before additional reinforcements arrived.

Running now at top speed, David could feel the adrenaline scorching his veins as it pumped through his body in lightning time. The pain became overwhelming as he opened his mouth and nose to gulp in air for emergency energy. Reaching the wall, he scrambled to the top, almost clawing his way over the brick enclosure.

The eugenia hedge on the opposite side cut into his skin, ripping his flesh as he clawed and stumbled his way through the sharp branches onto the cement pavement. He picked himself up, his entire body burning with cuts and bruises, his ankle twisted and swelling and hampering his escape.

Sirens, sirens, sirens, continued to blast from the distance. Ever closer, ever nearer, a constant reminder of his jeopardy. *Run*! he commanded his legs, aware of footsteps on the sidewalk.

Turning the corner, he saw his truck—and still another patrol car heading his way. Changing directions again, David half-ran, half-stumbled, his way along the street, aware of the surrounding homeowners watching this latest adventure in his life play out before them.

He wanted to scan them all, to send them back into their houses, but he hadn't the strength nor the opportunity. Though only a few minutes had passed since the mayor's murder, it seemed like hours, and his body was feeling the ache of his efforts to escape.

Reaching an alleyway lined with numbered trash bins awaiting collection, David charged forward, unsure of his destination. The large houses on either side of him stood as monuments to the wealth of their owners; his life-and-death struggle played out in their backyard like a surreal tragedy.

The police car turning into the alleyway behind him cut off any chance of retreat. His only possibility for escape must be ahead.

"Freeze!" a police megaphone sounded, only slightly louder than the beat of his heart inside his chest. "I said, freeze, dammit!" came the command again.

Suddenly, a shot rang out. The bullet was so close to David's head that he heard it as it whizzed by, hitting harmlessly into a trash can.

Angry now, David spun and fixed an instant scan on the policeman behind the wheel of the patrol car. Its tires screeched as the driver lost control, and the car spun in a ballet of metal and rubber, crashing into a row of trash cans and finally coming to rest against the stone wall of a mansion, blocking any entrance and exit from the alley. Inside, the unconscious forms of two patrolmen lay limp against the dash, their guns still drawn.

Half a mile away from the alley and its struggle for survival, a jeep headed in the direction of the sirens. Its driver was listening intently to a news report live from the scene.

"It's confirmed that gunshots have been fired in and around the residence of Mayor Franzoni," the reporter declared. "There is no indication whether the mayor is inside her house, or has been injured in the gunfire. All streets around the wealthy neighborhood have been blockaded with the entire police operation under the command of Lieutenant Guy Gelson."

David had no time to think of news broadcasts or journalists, so frantic was his effort to escape. Dashing in between several trash dumpsters, he wedged himself tight against the wall, hoping to escape detection. The wailing of the sirens around him were so piercing that they began to play havoc on his ability to concentrate.

Cupping his ears in semimadness, David prayed for relief from this purgatory of assault. His only chance of escape now was to keep a clear head, and his chances of maintaining that were decreasing with every moment.

A new noise—a motorcycle?—filled the air, heading his way. David was afraid to leave his temporary sanctuary, fearing certain discovery if he even budged. As the engine's roar became louder and the intruder closer, David could contain himself no longer.

Standing up quickly, he saw a motorcycle cop heading his way. The policeman hadn't noticed his prey half hidden by the trash container. Scanning quickly, scanning deadly, David telepathically ordered the policeman to accelerate his bike and direct it into the wall ahead. As the cop flew over the handlebars, David once again was on the run, having nowhere to hide and nowhere to find safety.

By the time he reached the far end of the alley, David was certain that cops would be swarming around him. Strangely, as he emerged, he was alone. While all the action continued to center a block away, David had his first opportunity in nearly an hour to sooth his nerves and calm his heart.

His clothes were drenched in sweat, dirty from the alley, and torn from his encounter with the thorny hedge. The bleeding cuts had crusted over in dried scabs which ached for medication and cleansing.

David knew his plan was a failure. The murder of the mayor had now turned him into a criminal even more wanted than before, and it had only served to increase Forrester's power. Continuing to walk, continuing to think, David found his mind so exhausted from the fight just finished that a good night's sleep was the only logical thought that kept recurring.

Any anticipation of rest was put quickly out of mind, however, when the spotlight of an undercover car parked across the street flashed in his face. Frozen in fear, David was shocked to see Drak step out and walk his way. He was not alone. Lieutenant Gelson was behind the wheel, and as Drak walked, Gelson slowly moved the patrol car to block the street—all the while keeping the glare of the searchlight in David's eyes.

David, trying to shield his eyes from the blinding light, could hear the incessant laughing of Drak who was propped up on the hood of the car.

"Hey, Davey," Drak called. "Time for a little one-on-one."

It was the last thing David needed to hear. He was almost ready to put his hands up in surrender, and let Forrester and Company do whatever they wanted with what remained of his body and mind.

"We're both scanners, Drak. Why help them," David shouted, trying to stall while hoping for a miracle. "They're going to use you and throw you away. You know it. You told me."

"And what're you going to do, Dave? Be my best friend?"

With the intensity of the bright spotlight eating at his brain, David felt a sudden snap of pain that drove right through his spine. Drak was scanning him and scanning him hard. David hardened to fight back, but found the blinding light hampering his defenses.

Drak poured on the pressure, his face contorting as his scan-tone reached a screeching pitch. Gnashing his teeth, David felt his face beginning to swell as the blood pulsed through his veins, pounding against his flesh.

He began to shudder violently at the tremendous force of Drak's scan, the pain in his head wiping away all sense of direction and reason. David was clearly losing this battle and he knew it. Yes, he was trying to fight; yes, he was concentrating all his remaining power against the attack. But nothing worked.

Staggering back, he felt his eyes beginning to bulge in his head, the pressure of the scan threatening to pop them from their sockets at any second.

"We can work together, all of us," David screamed in desperation. "Put our power to some decent use."

It was futile to appeal to Drak's sense of reason. Any that he had, had long ago disappeared in his addiction to EPH-2, and his fondness for inflicting pain.

"I like *this* use," Drak shouted back. "The power doesn't make you good, Davey. It just makes you powerful. And it makes me hungry. I'm gonna suck you dry, pretty boy."

And with that, Drak summoned up all his remaining power and concentrated it for one final blow. "Byebye. It's been a blast," he cackled at David from his position on the car's hood.

Paralyzed as if in a vice, David couldn't move, couldn't even blink his eyes, still blinded by the glare of Gelson's spotlight. The cruelty in Drak's scan was as deliberate as his sense of timing; he was dragging out the final seconds to feed his evil lust for power.

David felt his mind fading to a black nothingness. He wondered if this was the end. The exploding of his skull into a million specks of dust on a street in a city that was never his home.

He tried to fight back, but found himself falling to the ground, a beaten man without hope who wanted it to simply be over. Drak's nagging laughter in the background was almost more painful than the enormous pressure building in every corpuscle in his body.

"Byebye, Davey boy . . . Byebye, Davey boy . . . Byebye, Davey boy . . ." was droning in his head now, only slightly softer than a car engine's roar which seemed to be increasing in intensity. Rolling on his side, he saw the lights of a vehicle bearing directly down on him. Unable to move, paralyzed by the scan, his last thought was that he was about to be run over by a police car—the final irony in his battle against injustice.

Just as the vehicle was about to roll across his body, it swerved, with squealing tires and burning rubber, toward Gelson and his squad car.

The lieutenant had only a second to act, leaping out of the way of the vehicle just as it rammed into his trunk end, the impact sending Drak flying. It was an old jeep, immune to heavy damage, but capable of inflicting a crushing blow to the thin metal of the patrol car.

From his position on the ground, David could barely understand what was happening. He heard the crash and knew that somehow the scanning pressure had ended. Was he hallucinating, or was that Julie he saw running toward him.

As she ran to his side, his sister was appalled at what she saw. David was bleeding profusely from his ears, nose, and mouth. His clothes were nearly unrecognizable, covered in caked blood and dirt. "David," she said softly, trying to help him to his feet. "We've got to get out of here fast."

David rose weakly to his feet, hardly able to walk or see. With Julie as his guide, he felt himself being placed in the seat of the jeep. A moment later it was spinning its wheels out of the alley and out of danger.

Drak was not to be outdone. He pulled himself to his feet, screaming for Gelson to no avail. Rushing to the squad car, he found the lieutenant unconscious, covered in debris from a demolished trash dumpster. He turned quickly in an attempt to scan the fleeing jeep, but it was already too late, the vehicle's passengers too far in the distance for him to be effective.

"Damn you, Davey. I had you once, and I'll get you yet," he muttered to himself, clenching his fists in frustration.

The sun was already rising by the time David awoke to feel the cool wetness of a cloth upon his head. Julie was crouched nearby, watching her brother's every move.

"You've been asleep for hours, little brother," she smiled softly. "Must have had a hard day."

David winced as he remembered the reality of the past day. He was now lying inside what appeared to be a half-demolished building, broken furniture piled in the corner of the room. The strength of the sunlight coming through the broken windowpanes spelled early morning as David struggled to rise from his makeshift bed.

As he sat up, aware of an enormous headache, Julie smiled and threw him a bag from a fast-food restaurant. "Here," she laughed. "Eat your breakfast. We have a big day ahead of us."

David thanked God for having found his sister. More than his rescuer, she was his friend, and he knew it. "What do you mean?'' David asked, content to relax for hours or days.

"We have business," Julie said, losing her smile, her expression turning hard. "*Scanner* business."

He met her determined gaze and knew that he had gained a valuable partner in his fight.

CHAPTER NINE

REVENGE

"This is Brian Nace speaking to you from the newsroom of WVTV-TV. We have just received word that Mayor Franzoni has been assassinated at her estate in Luthmore Heights. Early reports indicate that the mayor was shot in the head with a high-powered rifle while at her desk located on the north side of her home. Police officers and the city's S.W.A.T. team have responded and have closed off the area.

A statement released by acting Police Commissioner Forrester's office denounced the shooting as 'senseless and insane.' According to earliest reports, the police are looking for escaped mental patient David Ketchum for questioning

*in connection with the case. It has been confirmed that he
was at the mayor's home at the time of the shooting.*

*"Reginald P. Kincaid, the mayor's longtime butler, is
said to be under sedation and unable to give a statement
at this time.*

*" 'We will not let the mayor's assassin remain free,'
Commissioner Forrester said in a formal statement. 'This
type of brutal and senseless act is more than a mere violation
of the law. It is a slap in the face of every law-abiding
citizen who had come to respect the mayor for her efforts
at cleaning up this community for our families and our
children. My police force will not stop until we apprehend
the murderer or murderers who committed this heinous
crime. On that you have my word.'*

"For WVTV-TV, this is Brian Nace."

The days since Alice had last seen David had turned
into moments of horror, slowly passing through her life,
not touching her directly, but rather affecting everything
around her.

The presence of that police officer named Carver in
her house, uninvited, was chilling enough, but being kept
a prisoner without ever having committed a crime was even
worse. Her every move and thought was centered around
the foreboding jailer who even now had his feet up on her
coffee table and was watching television in the living room.

As Alice kept herself busy breading chicken, she imagined how happy she would be to share this favorite family
recipe with David. Their first attempt at a home-cooked
meal had ended in death and tragedy. An involuntary shudder raced through her body as she remembered that night.

The sizzle from the frying pan, the sting as some fat
splattered on her fingers, brought Alice's mind back to her
kitchen and the task at hand. Breading chicken was an art,

she theorized, as she coated each piece individually in an egg and milk mixture and dredged it through some spiced bread crumbs before placing the individual parts of the plump bird neatly in the pan.

"Smells good. What's cooking?" Carver yelled from the living room, his question followed by a belch, and then another.

"Fried chicken, officer, sir," Alice responded with spunk, answering in a pleasant enough tone, though one tinged ever so slightly with hemlock. "Want some?" she invited, knowing full well there wasn't a police officer in the entire city who would turn down some homemade southern fried chicken.

"Sure. Why not?" Carver replied. It was the answer of one who was trying to remain aloof, somehow superior. Yet Alice knew if she listened really hard, the sound of his stomach grumbling for dinner would overpower even the television.

She walked slowly into the living room, her antenna directed toward Carver's stomach, honestly expecting to hear it growl. Instead, the news bulletin that came across the screen made her own stomach feel sick.

"David Ketchum, the man sought for the murder of Mayor Franzoni is a mental patient who has recently escaped from the hospital where he was being treated," the newscaster reported. On the screen, David's picture appeared, his innocent eyes sad and distant.

Carver chuckled to himself. The kind of wise-ass little laugh that made Alice want to slap his face just to hear the sound. But she was too stunned to react violently. The chill that threw its web across her body turned her hands to ice. She knew David could never have committed murder. He was obviously being framed.

Trembling, Alice stepped back into the kitchen, convinced that she had no choice but to go to David's defense. Quickly tying on a pair of jogging shoes, she silently and methodically walked to the stove, placed a potholder mitt on her right hand, and removed the steaming pot of soup that had been simmering all day.

"Come and get it!" Alice yelled as she backed behind the door.

As Carver walked whistling through the kitchen door, Alice whipped the pot of soup into his face. He never knew what hit him, the steaming liquid seared into his rough skin, burning it quickly and effortlessly.

Screaming in pain, Carver instinctively grabbed his face. He felt layers of skin peeling away, and then the shock of a knee planted firmly in his groin. A split second passed in which he was aware of the excruciating pain that would double him over. And then it hit. Cramping, aching, gut-wrenching agony that crippled the once cocky cop and left him vulnerable to Alice's next attack. A quick, sharp rap on the head with the empty pot, and Carver was a policeman on watch no more.

Moments after Alice was charging through her back door to freedom, Julie was quietly rolling her jeep to a stop under a clump of trees across from Dr. Morse's institute. As she silently cut her headlights, the horror of the place began to replay in her mind. Nodding bitterly, tears barely suppressed, Julie whispered, "That's the same place, all right."

David touched her hand, knowing full well the drama and heartache that vivid memories can bring. The fact that the institute and those inside caused their parents' death made his soul cry out all the more for revenge. And for Julie it could only be worse.

They silently watched the gate guards, who seemed to

be enjoying themselves. An occasional laugh would resound from the small kiosk, echoing across the hollow landscape. It was only when one of the guards emerged into the light that David recognized Gruner—uglier than ever in the reflected glow of the mercury lamp overhead.

"One of those guards is a scanner," David said to his sister, frowning. "He'll be impossible to get past."

Julie thought quietly for a moment, and then slowly turned to face David. The look in her eyes was serious; almost frightening.

"Before he died, Dad taught me a trick," Julie confided. "We practiced a few times. I'm not sure I can even remember how. But, if you scan just right, you can get inside people's minds, look through their eyes, see what they see."

David didn't understand how something so impossible-sounding could possibly work. Even so, he realized that the very concept of scanning had been foreign to him before he heard about that. "Show me," he whispered, eager to learn more.

Julie looked worried. She wasn't at all certain that she even remembered the delicate scanning technique. Moreover, it was dangerous, her father had said. Still, it might be their only way into the institute.

Uncertain, she shook her head. "It's too risky," Julie decided finally. "And it probably wouldn't work anyway."

David was more determined now than ever. "I've got to get in there, Julie. Show me!" He could feel the stress tightening his throat, reflecting in his voice.

Julie didn't move. She remained silent as they both watched a car pass them on the bridge and drive quickly up to the institute's gates. After a brief moment the heavy gates parted and it drove through.

Julie's mind was racing. The sight of the institute had

brought to the surface feelings she had managed to suppress for twenty years. There was anger, of course. And hatred for what had been done to her parents. But most of all, she felt the frustration of allowing herself to remain helpless for all those years, never fighting, never challenging for an instant.

Instead of putting her own life on the line, she had chosen to remain silent, hiding from everyone and everything, alone in a mountain cabin. Secluded from the reality of life around her, she had deluded herself into apathy. It was a luxury she could no longer afford.

Knowing that her time to fight was now, Julie made up her mind. "Look at me," she said to her brother, her voice turning rough and exact. "Look into my eyes. And do as I say."

Their eyes met. David stared with anticipation, locked in place by the intensity of Julie's expression.

"Scan me lightly," she told him.

David hesitated for a moment, remembering the last time he had tried to scan Julie and the violent reaction it had caused. He started slowly, or at least that's what he thought.

"No, lighter," she said. "You can slip into my mind, but go very gently. I should hardly feel a thing."

David tried, but either he didn't know what he was supposed to do, or he lacked the finesse or something. In any case it wasn't working. He could tell Julie was disappointed.

"David. Don't give up," she stressed, never dropping her gaze for an instant. "Scan me again, but this time, think of going inside my mind. Think of it like a labyrinth that you must travel through to reach the other side."

David was trying. He couldn't feel her mind. He didn't see a labyrinth. Then suddenly, unexpectedly, there he was.

Even though he knew he was staring at Julie, what he was seeing was himself—through her eyes.

The sensation was incredible. It was like looking in a mirror, without a mirror. It required enormous concentration to maintain such a low scanning level, but the more he continued to scan through Julie's mind, the more comfortable he became with controlling the maneuver.

"You just turned into *me!*" David whispered, afraid if he talked too loudly his concentration would be broken. "This is wonderful!"

"It's because you're looking through my eyes, that's all," she said. As she turned her head forward, David was able to see out the front windshield of the jeep, despite the fact that he was still looking at Julie. It was hard to believe, even harder to continue, the necessary level of concentration being so intense.

David dropped his scan, unable to keep it up. He wasn't used to the pressure, and was uncomfortable with looking at what seemed like two places at the same time.

It was then that another car passed them on the road. David's heartbeats raced in recognition when he saw Gelson at the wheel. David instinctively crouched lower in the jeep.

"It's Gelson," David said to Julie, as they watched the car approach the gates. "He's Forrester's man; the one who probably killed the mayor."

"All right. Use him," Julie shot back, without emotion.

As Julie focused on David, David focused a scan on Gelson. He tried his best to barely penetrate his mind. The distance across the bridge and to the gate made his task all the more difficult.

The scan hit Gelson just as his car stopped at the gate. He felt the slightest tingle behind his eyes, like a nervous twitch. But one so subtle that he merely blinked it away.

"Hey, Lieutenant," Gruner said staring at Gelson, "something the matter?"

Gelson rubbed his eyes gruffly, without answering.

"Lighten up. Pull back," Julie said to David, aware that he was concentrating too hard. "Can you see?"

"No . . . ah, yes. Yes, I can see Gruner now." David was both amazed and thrilled at his newfound power as he watched through Gelson's eyes.

"Lieutenant?" Gruner asked again, startled to see Gelson's eyes turn a milky white. "You sure you don't need some help?"

"Open the gate, damnit," Gelson replied, now irritated and aggressive.

As Gruner hit the code to electronically open the gates, he couldn't help but wonder about Gelson's eyes and the strange change in their color. Then again, why should he care. He never liked Gelson much, he thought. A strange loner type.

Across the lawn inside the jeep, David was ecstatic. "He doesn't even know we're there," he said quietly to Julie. "What a trip. I can see the front of the institute now. He's pulling up outside the front door."

"Relax your control, David," Julie warned. "Let him go about his business."

For David, the feeling of being inside someone else's brain, inside someone else's body, was unlike anything he had ever experienced. Though he sat quite still in Julie's jeep, his mind was observing every detail as Gelson unbuckled his seat belt and headed toward the institute's front door.

The two armed guards at the front reception desk barely looked up as Gelson entered. He passed by them without speaking, walking down the main corridor toward Dr. Morse's office.

Then he abruptly turned and headed into the men's room, walking to the sink.

"Pull back, pull back," Julie warned. "We can't let him see his eyes."

David quickly ended his scan just as Gelson looked up into the mirror while he pulled some paper towels from the holder nearby.

He wet the towels with cold water and rubbed down his face, as though trying to snap himself out of what seemed like a trance. Staring once again in the mirror, he examined his teeth and smiled at his reflection, apparently pleased at his appearance.

"I gotta quit drinking," he muttered to himself as he tossed the wet towels in the trash can and plodded back out into the hallway.

Quite gently now, David scanned back into Gelson's mind. It came easier this time, as he slipped inside totally unnoticed. Not even the slightest tingling could be detected. Certainly Gelson didn't realize the difference as he smugly entered the elevator and pushed the button for the basement level.

As he exited, however, there was something robotic in his step, almost automaton in his appearance. Walking down the hallway, Gelson paused at every door, slowly opening each one and peering inside as if looking for something lost or forgotten.

Room after room were opened and examined, each as empty as the next. Gelson finally reached the end of the long, sterile hallway and faced a reinforced steel door; a giant shiny gray barrier emblazoned with the sign: "AUTHORIZED PERSONNEL ONLY—ABSOLUTELY NO ADMITTANCE." Gelson punched a code into the security box and the heavy metal door slid open.

"Remember that code," Julie instructed David, who just nodded his head in acknowledgement.

Stepping through the doorway, Gelson entered another long hallway, glassed in on either side. Walking slowly forward, Gelson peered through the glass on the left, into an empty holding tank.

Turning the opposite way, he walked with precise steps to the other side of the hallway and looked down once again. This time the holding tank was full.

The four captive degenerate scanners in the large padded cell below recoiled at the sight of Gelson's probing eyes. Two men and two women went crazy, like caged apes in a zoo, hooting and screeching at the top of their lungs.

"Some scanners," David said. "Or what's left of them."

One saucer-eyed scanner defiantly returned Gelson's stare. He was both the strongest of the bunch, and the most curious.

As Julie concentrated with David on the four hopelessly addicted scanners in the cell, she suddenly let out a muffled cry. "Oh my God, David. That's Walter down there. He's alive."

Her astonishment at seeing the fiancé she thought long dead was unnerving. David felt her hand trembling against his arm as he continued his constant scanning of Gelson.

The lieutenant was focused on the erratic behavior of the scanners in the holding tank. Walter continued to stare at Gelson while two of the others hovered against the walls, continually moving and crossing each other's paths. The fourth, a slender young woman, was squatting low in a far corner, fearing even to look up in Gelson's direction.

The sudden opening of the metal security door caused Gelson to spin in surprise.

"Lieutenant!" Dr. Morse yelled, stunning the silence of the hallway with his anger. "You know you're not permitted in this area. Ever!"

"I thought . . . I thought I heard something," Gelson replied, in an uncharacteristic monotone.

Morse reacted instantly. He recognized the walk; he recognized the speech. Moving quickly to Gelson's side, he stared into his eyes. The zombielike look from the lieutenant's gaze caused a chill to rush down Morse's spine.

Julie's eyes widened as she saw Morse approach through Gelson's eyes. Her old nemesis was suddenly back in view after all these years. She wanted to kill him; she had to fight the urge to do it there and then. Only David's pacifying scan managed to keep her in check.

"That louse. That human vermin," Julie spat in a stilted, far-off voice that David didn't recognize.

Her face took on a stonelike quality that resembled a wax mask, so intense was her concentration on her mortal enemy—the man who had taken her parents away.

"You'd better come with me," Dr. Morse was saying as he pulled an automatic pistol, giving the lieutenant very little choice.

Suddenly, Julie burst into a smile. She wouldn't let another opportunity slip by. "I've waited eight long years for this moment," she said, suddenly snapping her head up toward the sky.

When David felt her scan racing past his, he pushed forward into Gelson's mind. Harder and harder Julie concentrated. Stronger and stronger the scan became. Brother and sister united to destroy the very essence of evil that had claimed their parents.

Gelson's head involuntarily jerked up and his intense stare arrested Morse's eyes. The scan stopped him in his tracks; he was unable to move even the smallest muscle.

Morse was trapped by his own manipulation. Seized by excruciating pain, he tried to reach up and grab at his temples. The blood was pulsating through his veins at such a speed that capillaries began to break in rapid succession.

Dropping the gun and falling to his knees, he let out a scream that echoed through the institute. Crawling on hands and knees, trying to escape the ever strengthening scan, Morse felt the blood begin to stream from his nose and ears. He had to make it to his testing lab and safety. It was his only hope.

David and Julie were relentless, though, and Gelson followed Morse up the hallway, just far enough away to watch the cowering doctor. Blood was smeared up the hallway as Morse finally reached the lab door; he pushed through with a shriek that revealed the intense pain of bone crushing under the stress of expanding blood vessels.

He entered the room and was out of Gelson's—and David and Julie's—sight. His respite from the intensity of the scan was brief. As Morse took his first deep, full breath in over two minutes, Gelson burst through the door, blasting Morse with all the combined scanning power that Julie and David could muster.

"Stop! Please, God in heaven. Stop!" Morse pleaded, the blood now gushing out of his mouth and making speech almost impossible.

Gelson wasn't about to show Morse any mercy, even if he were in control of his actions. Something inside him was actually enjoying this show of scanning power.

With a sharp twist of his head, Gelson scanned Morse with a megablast which sent him flying across the room, smashing into a racks of needled EPH-2 syringes. As the racks came crashing to the floor, the sound of the breaking glass and twisted metal did little to camouflage Morse's pleading for mercy.

Again David and Julie increased the scan; again Morse was tossed across the room like a rag doll. The one-time physician and saviour of lives was being reduced to a bloody, mangled mound of flesh.

Harder and harder Julie concentrated, dragging David's scan along with her. The expression of triumph in her face was obvious as she saw the physical destruction she wrought.

"Let's give the doctor a taste of his own medicine," she hissed, almost out of control now.

She clenched her fists and gritted her teeth and sent a scan through Gelson's eyes that made David's blood begin to boil. The scan-burst was so intense that Gelson's nose began to bleed as well. It blasted Morse once again across the room, smashing him into the fallen rack of EPH-2 syringes.

Dozens of needles simultaneously popped from their cartridges, each injecting the nearly unconscious doctor with lethal fluid. A hundred deadly needles full of EPH-2 pierced his flesh and entered his bloodstream.

Morse staggered to his feet, shuddering violently. The veins in his arms began to pop open and bleed, spurting out arcs of blood with each beat of his heart. He turned blue at first and then a vile shade of green, unable even to scream as he took his final breath.

Only Julie and David were fully aware of the irony of his death: he lay silent and convulsing near the same laboratory table where he had taken so many lives.

Julie triumphantly broke her scan and fell back in the seat of her jeep, a broad smile on her lips. She took a deep breath, proud of her and her brother's work.

"Wait, there's someone!" David called out, still maintaining his scan of Lieutenant Gelson.

The lab door burst open, and Gelson whirled around.

Drak was looming at the door. The scanner merely grinned maniacally, an embodiment of evil.

"Knock, knock. Is that you in there, Davey?" he asked in mock seriousness.

Suddenly, Drak reversed the process, scanning Gelson in a vicious attack against David. The helpless lieutenant screamed as the two opposing scans met head-on inside his skull. His brain seemed to expand under the pressure; his head jerked violently out of control.

Clawing at his cheeks and then his temples, Gelson was unable to withstand the intensity of the fight going on inside his head. Screaming for relief, the once swaggering police officer was reduced to an immobile mass, seething with pain.

As the high-pitched scan-tone reached the outer limits of human hearing, Drak was in his glory. "This is fun. Like playing with a puppet," he mocked, walking closer to Gelson. All the better to enjoy the show.

Caught in Drak's massive attack, David was thrown against his seat, unable to concentrate because of the pain. Shuddering uncontrollably, he grabbed Julie's arm for support.

"David, *let me!*" she responded, reactivating her scan to fight Drak's.

Drak was scanned back away from Gelson and toward the door. Not about to be beaten, he fought back, concentrating his scan while screaming David's name.

"Davey! Davey! Davey!" he repeated in maddening succession.

Gelson's head was jerking, back and forth, involuntarily. Blood gushed from his ears as he screamed for mercy to anyone who would listen. He would never know that he was merely a pawn in a deadly game of one-upmanship.

As Gelson turned to face Drak and tried to step toward

the door, his brain began to smolder from within. The very gray matter started cracking through his skull, bloating under the pressure of the scan. Then, in a violent fiery burst, his entire head exploded, sending pieces of flesh splattering across the room.

Even before Gelson's headless body hit the floor, Drak was out the door. "You're dead, Davey," he growled, running toward the elevator, his words echoing down the corridor behind him.

CHAPTER TEN

ETERNITY

The blares of various alarms screaming to life all at the same instant snapped David back to the present. His face was beaded with sweat; his entire body damp from perspiration.

It was as if he had been in a horrible dream, or in that eerie place that is neither awake nor asleep but somewhere in between. He was shaking in Julie's arms as he opened his eyes to the reflection of search lights scanning the institute grounds. It was as if war had been declared, he thought. He was more right than he ever would have guessed.

"What happened?" David asked, his head feeling like a thousand oxen had trampled his brain. "What's going on?" he said, sitting up in his seat and looking to Julie for some sense of the situation.

"Just hold on." As she mouthed the words, she downshifted into first gear and floored the accelerator on her jeep. The four-wheel drive vehicle leapt from its hiding place and onto the road.

Gruner and the other security guard were already on alert. The continuing alarms had seen to that. The squeal of tire rubber on asphalt only heightened their senses.

They raced from the gate house but were one beat too slow to realize what was happening. The beam of the jeep's headlights was already upon them. They had only seconds to think, even less time to react.

Before they could move from the spot, the front grill of the speeding jeep smashed into their bodies, throwing them twenty feet into the air. Gruner landed first, crashing into the guard booth. The other guard was less lucky, breaking his neck in the fall.

Shifting into reverse and then back to first gear, Julie gunned the accelerator once again. The jeep charged the closed gates, smashing through the perimeter of the institute's grounds. David was barely able to hold onto the jeep's grab-handle and remain seated, so forceful was the jolt when they cleared the gates. They made their way quickly up the institute's drive, steam pouring from under the hood, and pulled alongside the main building.

Even before Julie cut the headlights, David was out of the jeep and running toward the front door.

"David! Get down!" Julie shouted after him, sensing trouble ahead.

The words had hardly left her lips when a security

guard with a submachine gun emerged from the bushes nearby and began firing. David rolled to escape the bullets. Then he was up and lunged behind a parked car, with Julie following behind.

The sound of the bullets was deafening as slugs hit the thin metal and pierced the car's outer flesh. David and Julie just waited for the firing to stop, knowing that the guard would need a fresh clip soon, so rapidly was he firing.

A second and third security guard ran out the front door—one armed with a tranquilizer gun, the other with a pistol. As they raced to join their comrade, the first guard was reloading, and quietly heading toward David.

Lying half hidden underneath the car, Julie knew she only had seconds to act. Grabbing a piece of broken rear-view mirror, she reflected a scan at the guard with the submachine gun, concentrating her power to stop him in his tracks.

As the power of the scan invaded his mind, the guard turned suddenly and headed back toward the other men rushing toward him. His eyes were like a zombie's; his mind was totally controlled by another. Blood began to drain from his nose and ears as the scan-tone pierced the air around him.

Unconsciously, but with deadly aim, he lowered his submachine gun and began to fire at the oncoming guards, sending one rolling to the ground in a defensive maneuver. The other guard was hit squarely in the chest; the bullets collapsed his lungs and sent him staggering backwards. It was more by chance than by accuracy that the single shot he was able to fire struck the scanned guard in the skull, killing him instantly.

The silence that followed was staggering. With the barrage of bullets still echoing in her head, Julie pulled herself past David and out from underneath the car. She assumed all three guards were dead, and was too quick, too careless, with her movements.

"Julie, no!" David screamed, but not in time.

The guard with the tranquilizer gun fired a dart which hit David's sister squarely in the back. David raced from safety into the open, grabbing the dart and yanking it out quickly. In a single movement, he spun and scanned the remaining guard mercilessly, blasting him with a furious scan-burst, sending portions of the man's body into the shrubbery nearby.

Despite David's speed, the drug was already beginning to take its toll on Julie's body; her strength was ebbing. Fighting to stand and losing the battle, Julie stumbled back behind the car. David rushed to her.

"Go on . . . help Walter," she gasped, trying not to use precious breath.

"Stay right here. I'll be back," David assured her. Not wanting to leave, but knowing he must, David rolled his jacket in a tight ball and placed it under Julie's head as her eyes closed and she fell into a heavy sleep.

His mind racing, David made his way quickly through the side door of the institute, aware that his life might end at any moment. His heartbeat was so intense that the fabric of his shirt was actually vibrating with its rhythm.

As David ran through the now-empty main reception area and turned the corner toward the long, antiseptic corridor, another security guard began charging in his direction. Suddenly, the events seemed to be happening in slow-motion—the ominous uniformed guard hurtling toward him; the submachine gun at his side being armed and aimed; the look of death in the man's eyes.

"Hold your fire!" David yelled, hitting the guard with a scan-burst.

It was like hitting the *pause* button on a video recorder. The charging guard simply froze in place. A figure frozen in action, scanned into submission with a single glance.

Suddenly, the guard began to move again. More slowly now, as if in a trance. "Oh, Jesus," he said. "I'm sorry! I didn't recognize you, Commissioner Forrester."

It was just a theory, but it had worked. David knew that if he could scan into people's minds, even to the point of entering their brains and visualizing through their eyes, that he also should be able to make them hallucinate. Not wildly; not unpurposefully; but with a specific intent. In this case, he had become Commissioner Forrester to this poor, confused guard.

"Go home, you idiot! Get out of here!" David said, even sounding like Forrester, adopting his insensitive attitude.

Without any questions, the guard dropped his weapon and walked robotlike down the corridor and out the front door.

Across town, the real police commissioner was rather impressed. Forrester was in front of a mirror, dressed in a tux, starched formal shirt, with his hair slicked back, smiling at his reflection. He was certainly fit for his age, he thought. Elegant, powerful, and mediagenic. But his smile wasn't to last long.

First came the intrusion of his press liaison. "Sir, we have to leave. I've arranged an interview before the reception."

Next came the sound of the office intercom, and with it the words that spelled another potential disaster in the making. "Excuse me, sir . . . there's been an emergency."

Not Forrester's favorite phrase. His face reflected his anger as he picked up the telephone to learn all the details.

As Forrester was receiving the news of the incident at the institute, David was already nearing the walkway above the scanner's holding tank. The secret code he had remembered from Gelson paid off now as he slipped quickly through the heavy reinforced security door and walked toward the one-way window.

The hallway was covered in blood, left over from Gelson's possessed scanning of Dr. Morse. The bloody footprints heading toward the laboratory remained, a gruesome souvenir of death.

Looking through the window, down into the scanner pit, David recognized Walter. The scanner still retained some strength compared to the other addicts in the cell. Raising his hand to get Walter's attention, David was first aware of the sudden pain throbbing through his temples; then of the presence of someone else in the hallway.

David spun around, the blood already running from his nostrils, and was face-to-face with Feck, whose silly grin distorted his face. The tranquilizer gun his enemy held was leveled and armed.

"What's the matter, Davey. Little nosebleed?" he mocked.

Feck, a little too self-assured, a little too slow, tightened his finger on the trigger. It was the last move he would voluntarily make.

David scanned quickly in response, and was able to hold his attacker at bay. Even as Feck continued straining to pull the tranquilizer gun's trigger, David turned up the pressure. Like a torrential wind, he forced Feck back, faster and faster, toward the far end of the corridor.

The tranquilizer gun clattered to the floor as Feck was driven with such force into the far wall that the imprint of his body was smashed into the plaster. As he fell face-first onto the floor, the blood drained from his ears, and lent fresh witness to the destruction occurring there.

Exhausted by the effort to subdue Feck, David turned and collapsed against the window, his breathing labored, his mind once again on the scanners below. He had to reach them and somehow explain that he was their friend. It wouldn't be an easy assignment.

Time was short. Any moment another guard could charge in his direction. More important, this group of four scanners were hopelessly addicted to EPH-2, which made them unpredictable. Caged together for these many months, there was no telling how they would react to help from a stranger. Worse still, he dared not use scanning on them. Causing the four prisoners the slightest pain would not help convince them of his sincerity.

"Not bad, pretty boy."

The sound of Drak's voice hissing down the hallway and into David's brain like a wicked memory caught David off guard. David spun on his heels, turning to face his enemy. Too slow, too late. With a single merciless scan, Drak's energy exploded through David's body. He flew backward and crashed through the window.

As David hit the glass, his mind could think only of death. Not his, but the scanners' below, who were caught in the rainfall of splintered glass as he plummeted the fifteen feet to the floor. The glass showered the room; the scanners screamed in horror.

David hit the floor hard. For a second he dared not move, not quite knowing if he were alive or dead. His mind was locked into a dazed blank state where nothing mattered—neither pain nor escape.

Drak's malicious laughter from the floor above snapped him back to attention, however. It was the gloating victory cackle of one who knew too little to be afraid, one too presumptuous to be defensive.

"I'll be right down, Davey, and we can start with appetizers," he laughed, disappearing into the corridor.

It was Walter who moved first, coming to David's side and helping him to his feet. It was then that the first shock of pain registered throughout his body. His left arm was obviously broken, and the agony from the injury was just beginning.

"Thank you," David uttered gently, looking appreciatively into Walter's eyes. "Your name is Walter, isn't it?"

"Yes." The man's voice was tinged with amazement. "But who are you?"

"David Ketchum. Julie Vale is my sister."

Walter's face lit up in recognition. It was wonderful to see life return, if only for a moment, into eyes which had long shared only isolation. "Julie!" he exclaimed, smiling the look of one recalling pleasant memories of a life past.

"She's outside right now. We came to help you. All of you," David said, turning to include the others. They were cowering together in a far corner, as much distrustful of the newcomer as of each other. "Go ahead, look at me. See what I am doing?" he told them, beginning to scan across the room.

He knew he had only seconds before Drak would burst through the holding-cell door. He knew that he must act now to recruit what life was left in these addicts. Turning to Walter, he pleaded for help. "Scan me and show them you still know how."

"I don't know if. . . ." Walter began, obviously trying to remember what had once come so naturally.

Slowly David began to feel the familiar tingle of a

weak scan inside his mind. "Yes, YES!" he shouted in jubilation. "You can all do it, if you just try," he said, once again involving the entire room.

Two scanners came forward, but the fourth and weakest grabbed for a syringe of EPH-2.

"Quit killing yourself," David shouted, racing to knock the needle from the scanner's grasp.

"But I need it. I'm in pain," the degenerate meekly said as he turned his head away from David in shame.

"Endure it," David said, feeling no compassion now. "Don't be afraid. If we all stick together, we can get out of here. But we have to fight."

The sound of Drak kicking the door open frightened the spark of courage beginning to develop in the sorrowful-looking bunch.

"Nobody's going anywhere," Drak snarled, aware of his power over these pathetic creatures. "This the big feed, baby," he said, spinning to face David. He threw his head back in laughter, his cackle reverberating through the room.

David seized the opportunity. Clenching his fists and ignoring his own pain, he tried to scan Drak. The sound of the madman's laughter propelled him onward, but his weakened condition left him with little strength.

With a cruel, twisted snarl, Drak snapped his head in David's direction and slammed him to the floor with a single swift scan. David screamed in pain as he landed on his broken arm, helpless to defend himself any longer.

"Julie!" he cried, projecting his thoughts to his sister outside.

Lying very still next to the bullet-ridden car in the institute's parking lot, Julie felt David's plea for help. Call it instinct; call it bonding; she knew her brother was in serious trouble—that was about to get worse.

Even as Julie clung to the hope that David would some-how summon the strength to escape, Forrester's car was pulling up the institute's driveway, followed closely by two police cars. Though their sirens were silenced, their twirling red lights turned the institute's exterior into a psychedelic show of eerie shapes and colors.

As Forrester leapt from his car, four policemen did likewise, jumping into step behind him as he entered the building.

"Find him and kill him!" Julie heard Forrester saying as the door slammed behind him and all was quiet again. Never had she felt so helpless or so afraid.

In the holding cell in the basement, Drak was enjoying his moments of glory. Like a circus performer in the center ring, he held his audience captive. This audience was dif-ferent, of course—one whose very life was in the balance.

Pinned to the floor by the strength of Drak's scan, David could not move. He found it difficult to breathe and impossible to concentrate.

"I'll finish you now, like I did your loving mother," Drak snarled, turning up the intensity of his scan, slowly, deliberately.

"You bastard," David screamed, horrified at the evil Drak could perform without conscience.

Drak appeared even more satisfied, having revealed his secret. His eyes pulsed with the energy his destruction de-livered. He actually was enjoying watching David unravel before his eyes, layer by layer of life slipping away.

Never before in his life had he felt such power over mankind. Now, instead of being the freak, the one looked down upon, Steven Drak was king. The years of teasing and abuse by all those around him poured forth through his scan, releasing the hurt and funnelling it toward another.

Drak was the happiest he could ever remember being at that very moment.

As Drak was about to deliver his death scan, a final crushing blow of telepathy, he was blocked by Walter who stepped into his gaze.

"Out of my way, you fool," Drak yelled, scanning right through Walter to get to David. It scalded Walter's very soul, so intense was Drak's power. He cried out and tumbled backward onto David.

The remaining three scanners watched in cowering helplessness, but they felt a mounting sense of outrage at the horror occurring before them. Still, they were weak compared to Drak's overwhelming strength.

As Drak delivered his final scan-burst, David began to writhe in pain. Too overcome to even scream, he began to silently tremble with preseizure intensity.

The degenerates suddenly came to David's defense. They wailed with surprising defiance. Clenching their fists as they had seen David do, they pooled their scanning power toward Drak to attract his attention.

He felt the jolt smacking his mind with the impact of a small electric shock. Nothing grand, nothing overwhelming, but enough to distract him for the briefest of seconds.

Seeing Drak's eyes roll to the back of his head, Walter rolled free of David, adding his own scan to the three other degenerates'. Pooling their strength together, they began to have an effect. Drak spun to face the trio of scanners.

With his back to David, Drak's defenses were down. As the four scanners held the madman in a vise of resurgent telepathy, David used the moment to roll free and add his scan to theirs. The impact was immediate.

Drak began to shudder first; then writhe, as he lost his

dominance. He tried to force them back by using intimidation, but to no avail. The combined strength of five against one made fighting impossible.

"No . . . agh . . . no," he screamed refusing to believe that he could be caught in such a trap.

As David and the scanners slowly formed a circle around Drak, searing him with their scanning, hitting him from all sides, he was forced down to the grill in the middle of the room.

His body was flailing about in an involuntary seizure; he was incapable of retaliation. His screams became muffled as blood poured out of his mouth and nose; his fetal position was a pathetic sign of submission.

The degenerates converged on Drak from all sides now, pulsing with reborn power. Their minds remembered what it was like to control, and they were as addicted to that sensation as they were to EPH-2.

They poured on their scanning strength as David stepped back to watch. Drak's entire body was beginning to bloat now. It was actually smoldering from the intensity of the electrifying energy blistering through it, on the verge of spontaneous combustion.

Drak let out one final bloodcurdling scream; his veins began to explode through his skin, his temples began to crack under the pressure from within. His entire body was enveloped in electrical scan-fire, which blazed even stronger than the bright light of the holding cell.

His steaming blood began to flow from every pore like lava from a volcano. His very face began to melt, to disintegrate before the scanners' eyes.

Despite his hatred for the man, David was unable to watch the unearthly horror before him. He turned just in time to miss the destruction of Drak's body—a horrible sucking inward of flesh and organs before exploding across the room. Body parts spattered everywhere; yet the release of evil somehow felt clean.

Forrester was stunned as he watched Drak's painful defeat on one of the monitors in Morse's office. His face was distorted now, like a madman unable to control his own destiny. Terrified, he staggered back, still maintaining his vigil of the screen.

Shifting his attention to another screen, the sight before him made his stomach retch. "This can't be . . ." he muttered, all too well aware that his battle was lost.

The view from the monitor canvassing the gate was dense with vans and camera crews arriving *en masse*. They were unloading from their vehicles like assault troops taking a position in war. The decimated front gate was no longer visible, so many were their number.

Like a dictator refusing to admit that his power base was gone, Forrester squared his tie and walked calmly toward the institute's front door. His mind raced through varying scenarios as he took the elevator ride to the ground floor.

He paused to wipe the perspiration off his brow, and then exited the building, looking every bit in charge, every bit at ease. He would not allow the media to invade the scene of his crimes, he decided. There was no way that his empire could be crumbling now.

In the front row, Alice stood proudly next to investigative reporter Brian Nace, her friend who had convinced his colleagues that her hysterical and incredible tale of horror at the institute was true.

The cameras rolled, their tapes recording every action, and newsmen surrounded the front entrance. Carole White spoke first. "Commissioner Forrester. What's happening here?" Her tone was full of accusation.

In answer, Forrester summoned the four patrolman around him. "Clear the area immediately!" he barked, refusing to show any sign of weakness. "Disperse or you'll all be placed under arrest!" he threatened, after none of the press began to move.

"Is it true that you have been using psychics called scanners?" another press person yelled from the crowd.

"That is a myth. Scanners are not real. There is no such thing," he shouted back, again repeating his threat of arrest. "Disperse, I said. Immediately."

The reporters were unmoved. They sensed Forrester was lying and knew he was nervous.

"What is your response to allegations that you deliberately assassinated criminals to gain popularity?" White shouted out from the front lines.

Forrester bristled at the accusation while the press muttered among themselves about the implications of such a charge.

"Nonsense. We've just captured the mayor's assassin inside this building," Forrester insisted. Wiping the sweat from his brow, he added, "His name is David Ketchum!"

The press met Forrester's statement with boos and hisses of resentment. It didn't take a genius to know Forrester was grasping at air in an attempt to divert attention from himself. Frantically, he looked around at his patrolmen for support. None stepped forward to stand at his side.

"Commissioner Forrester. We've learned that David Ketchum is *not* an escaped mental patient as you earlier suggested. In fact, he may actually be one of these 'scanners' you say do not exist. Could you comment?" attacked Nace.

"Ketchum's a maniac. There's no such thing as a scanner."

This was too much for Alice to stand. Pushing past Nace toward the front, she was nearly hysterical. "You're a liar. And a murderer!" she shrieked, losing all control.

Forrester was furious. Alice must have been responsible for this turnout. She surely was the ringleader, he surmised.

"Are you telling us that one person, this David Ketchum, is responsible for all this?" White asked, gesturing to the destruction and dead bodies still clearly visible.

"Of course not," Forrester responded. "Ketchum had accomplices. Drug addicts. They're inside. You'll see," he said, clearly beginning to panic.

Again, Alice could not remain silent. Someone had to hear the truth! "Why don't you come clean, Forrester. Enough of your alibis," she heckled.

Forrester pointed a finger in her direction, his entire body shaking with anger. "That girl is one of them! Arrest her," he directed his men.

Two patrolmen instinctively obeyed his command, rushing up to Alice. Backing away out of fear, she stumbled and fell. In a matter of seconds, the cops were upon her.

Struggling to free herself from their rough grasp, she screamed to be released. Forrester looked jubilant that he still had loyal members among the police force. Perhaps now the press would be more tolerant of his position.

The smile on his face was short-lived as a piercing scan hit him. Gasping for breath, unable to speak, he felt blood running from his nose. He turned, all too well aware that there must be a scanner in the crowd, and spotted Julie, standing alongside the bullet-ridden car. She was still groggy, but awake enough to handle Forrester, her eyes on fire with hatred for what he had said about her brother.

The press, unaware of the scan, were perplexed by

Forrester's behavior. The snapping of his head and his short-
ness of breath made it appear as he if were having a heart
attack.

"No, I won't . . . Stop it!" Forrester screamed, as if
being controlled by a foreign force.

The patrolmen attempting to handcuff Alice were as
confused as the press, uncertain if they should race to the
commissioner's aid or follow his orders to arrest the girl.
They wouldn't have to wait long for an answer.

In an attempt to escape Julie's scan, Forrester leapt
from the steps onto the crowded lawn of the institute. As
he tried frantically pushing past the cameramen and news
reporters, he was stunned by what he saw—

In front of him, mixed among the press, was David
Ketchum. At his side was Julie's fiancé Walter. Battle-
weary, but still able to scan, the two locked into Forrester's
crazed mind.

"No . . . it's not true," he screamed. "It's not!"

"David!" Alice shouted, seeing her boyfriend in the
crowd. "David," she screamed again, ripping free of the
police and racing toward him.

Alice wasn't the only one to see an old boyfriend
among the throngs of onlookers. "Walter?" Julie asked out
loud, touched to see her long-lost fiancé so near at last.

The press closed in for a closer look, surrounding
Forrester. Gritting his teeth, he fought the continuing scans,
refusing to give in, yet having very little choice. "Stop
them . . . Arrest them!" he shouted to no one in particular.
"No, I *won't!* Go away . . . No, shut up . . . SHUT UP!"
he screamed, becoming incoherent.

The sound of an approaching siren caused the entire
crowd to turn as one. The flashing lights atop the car added
still more of a circus feel to the bizarre scene. Vice Commissioner Yancy leapt from the car, as two of Forrester's

patrolmen attempted to brief him on the latest chaotic and incoherent developments as best they could.

Yancy's face became a study in hardness as the events of the past few hours were explained to him. The strange behavior of Lieutenant Gelson; Dr. Morse's bloody demise; Gruner, Feck, and Drak all dead; at least a dozen security guards killed or wounded.

The horror in Yancy's eyes became ever more evident as he watched Forrester's continuing struggle for survival before him. David and Walter could not let the police commissioner escape the consequences of his deeds. They strengthened their scan, concentrated even harder.

The pain was too much for Forrester to bear. He knew his moment of surrender had arrived. Falling to his knees, begging for mercy, he broke down before the throng. "All right. All right. I'll say it," he blurted out, holding his head in pain.

"Say what, Commissioner," Yancy asked.

"Everything. Everything. But I *had* to do it . . . to save the order . . . the new order . . . the *future*!"

"We don't understand, Commissioner Forrester," newswoman White queried, continuing the pressure from the media.

He didn't want to answer, but a snap of David's head in a scan-burst gave him little choice.

"Aagh!" Forrester cried in torment. "All right. I ordered . . . Chief Stokes killed . . . the mayor scanned . . . then . . . murdered!"

Two policemen moved in at Yancy's direction to handcuff the police commissioner. He pulled himself away, attempting unsuccessfully to stand. "You have to understand. I only did it to save the city. Maybe the way I went about it was wrong, but the idea, the idea . . ."

With that, Forrester collapsed to the ground barely

conscious as the scans were dropped. His body twitched involuntarily; he was injured but alive.

Alice could only look into David's eyes with a sense of relief and deep gratitude. He had done more than save the city from an invasion of mind-control fanatics; he had freed future generations of scanners to use their power for freedom and to help others.

"David, thank God!" she said when she finally spoke, the words catching in her throat as tears of happiness streamed down her face.

There was a visible sigh of pleasure as David hugged Alice gently favoring his broken arm, content at last in himself and who he was. As Yancy and his officers pulled Forrester to his feet, David watched, full of pity for the deranged policeman. Perhaps somewhere in his demented mind, he actually did think he was trying to help others. It was hard to imagine.

Forrester suddenly caught David's look of benevolence. It was more than Forrester could bear.

"You!" he screamed, shaking loose his police guard and pulling his .44 revolver from his tuxedo. Before anyone could react, he aimed it at David and pulled the trigger.

"Down!" David shouted, pushing Alice to the ground and falling right beside her.

Forrester's shot went wild, hitting the side of a video camera and embedding itself in the viewfinder. Before Forrester could get off another round, David scanned his mind hard, no longer caring about compassion or redemption.

Julie and Walter joined in retaliating against the pathetic lawman who didn't know when to quit. He had overplayed his moment, and would now pay the price.

Revenge, built up over decades, came pouring forth as their triple scan sent Forrester's blood to the boiling point.

His entire body quaked with the power of the seizure the scan brought. Not even the pair of policemen who came rushing back to Forrester's side could control the convulsions.

The collected press gasped in amazement as cameras continued to record the all-out attack on the madman. Scantones filled the air, causing video levels to peak and soundmen to remove their headsets.

Forrester shuddered as his neck and head swelled in bloated size. His bow tie fell to the ground and his collar split open under the pressure. His cheeks ballooned to grotesque proportions, and his eyes enlarged in his skull, threatening to pop out of their sockets.

The horror of the moment was too much for many and they turned their eyes away from the gruesome reality of the power of scanners.

"Kill him!" Walter screamed, encouraging the others to join him in one last grand scan-blast.

"No," said David, returning to his senses and attempting to calm the others. "We're not like him. And we will never be."

At last, Yancy drew his .38 and stopped the scanning at its peak. There had been enough killing in this place without yet another death. "You're under arrest, 'sir,' " he sneered in disgust at Forrester, who was too far gone to even realize what was happening.

As David and Alice turned once again, they noticed the stares from the surrounding press. Convinced of the scanners' power, yet unsure of their control, they hesitated to move or to speak.

Feeling their insecurity, David said, "We mean no one any harm. We only want to help."

As they walked to their car, David and Alice were joined by Julie and Walter, uncertain of their future, but sure of their loyalty to one another. The life of a scanner would never be easy. But perhaps, just perhaps, they could use their gift in gentle, healing ways to help mankind and themselves as well.

And in an alley across town, a solitary black cat searched the decaying trash from the Twin Dragon All-Nite Chinese Emporium, unaware that it had been a witness to history. And a saga that continues still.